MEET

Fortune o

Age: 29

Vital Statis____ Dirty-blond hair, blue eyes, miles of muscles. He's very private, maybe a little shy. And he's got a secret.

Claim to Fame: One of the Florida Fortunes, recently relocated, he's a wealthy contractor with a lot to lose.

Romantic Prospects: If you ask him, he's not in the market. His life is complicated enough already.

Rambling Rose was supposed to be just another stop on the road for the Fortunes—and, to be honest, I feel we have already overstayed our welcome. I've tried to convince my brothers it's time to go.

But now there is Hailey. She's…an angel. And she wants me. It would be so easy to say yes. But she has no idea what the world can be like, how you can start out with the best of intentions and everything can still go so wrong. I should go before things get complicated. Before I have to choose between the perfect woman and the secret daughter I would do anything for…

Dear Reader,

Once upon a time there was a shy little Polish girl in Salvation Army shoes who loved to read. Books (and old movies on a black-and-white TV) were her best and only friends. Because of them, she learned how to speak English (not her first, or her second, language). Since she loved Westerns, she twanged a little when she spoke, something the other kids made fun of. They also made fun of her secondhand clothes. Even so, she was determined to get other kids to like her, but she didn't know how. All she had were her books and the stories she made up to entertain herself—and her determination to make friends.

One spring day in the schoolyard at recess, the little girl started telling a story about a large family in the 1800s traveling west in a covered wagon, and something wonderful happened. The kids around her started to listen. Not only that, but when recess was over (and the story was far from through), they asked if she was going to continue telling the story the next day! Suddenly, she knew what she wanted to do with the rest of her life. She wanted to entertain people because they not only noticed her then, but they seemed to like her, as well.

And that's how my career path came about. That was in the fifth grade. I still remember the title of that "epic" story (although very little else), *Anna Marie Anders: Adventurous Girl*. It's been a long road from there to here, but I am very happy I never gave up. I still love telling stories.

As always, I thank you for picking up one of my books to read, and from the bottom of my heart I wish you someone to love who loves you back.

All the best,

Marie Ferrarella

Fortune's Greatest Risk

Marie Ferrarella

HARLEQUIN

SPECIAL
EDITION

Special thanks and acknowledgment are given
to Marie Ferrarella for her contribution to
the Fortunes of Texas: Rambling Rose continuity.

Recycling programs
for this product may
not exist in your area.

USA TODAY bestselling and RITA® Award–winning author **Marie Ferrarella** has written more than two hundred and fifty books for Harlequin, some under the name Marie Nicole. Her romances are beloved by fans worldwide. Visit her website, marieferrarella.com.

Books by Marie Ferrarella

Harlequin Special Edition

Forever, Texas

Matchmaking Mamas

The Fortunes of Texas: The Lost Fortunes

The Fortunes of Texas: The Secret Fortunes

The Montana Mavericks: The Great Family Roundup

Visit the Author Profile page at Harlequin.com for more titles.

To
Charlie
Whose Kisses Still
Make the World
Fade Away.

Prologue

If anyone would have said to him seven months ago that twenty-nine was far too old for someone to actually feel homesick, Dillon Fortune would have laughed them off. In his opinion, being homesick was an emotion associated with preteens who were spending a month or so away from home surrounded by a bunch of strangers at a sleepaway camp for the very first time.

And yet, here he was, a grown man, feeling a deep, penetrating wave of homesickness.

Granted, he had been in Texas for more like seven months. And, yes, instead of being alone amid a bunch of strangers, he'd come out here with two of his brothers, Callum and Steven, as well as one of his sisters, Stephanie. But, when all things were considered, he had to admit, if only to himself, that he was most definitely homesick.

Very homesick.

Yes, Rambling Rose, Texas, was a beautiful place as well as an up-and-coming, flourishing town. A town that he and his brothers were heavily involved in building up, thanks to the construction company that the three of them owned. But if anyone would have asked him, Dillon would have had to say that his heart was back in Fort Lauderdale, Florida.

Dillon wished that the rest of him could be back there, as well.

But he had always been raised to believe that commitments, especially to family, came first and he couldn't very well just take off for Fort Lauderdale now, even though he really wanted to. He was committed to these various projects. His brothers were counting on him and he knew he couldn't just leave before all the projects were completed and up and running.

Granted, the new pediatric center and the veterinary clinic were now both open and successful. The pediatric center had even been christened, so to speak, on its very first day. A pregnant woman—Laurel, last name unknown—had gone into labor during the clinic's ribbon-cutting ceremony. She was quickly rushed to a hospital in San Antonio with a NICU just in time, and gave birth there.

But the same success story couldn't be written about The Shoppes at Rambling Rose, a collection of high-end stores which were built on the site of what had once been the town's five-and-dime.

Not that any of the shops had failed—it was too soon to say something like that—but so far, they hadn't been able to find their dedicated audience yet, people who could be seen as a loyal clientele. He had no doubts that that would happen—Callum had a knack for picking places that were just *waiting* to become successes. But Dillon had no desire to remain here waiting for that magical moment to transpire.

This part, he thought, could easily go on without him.

Yet here he was, sitting in his car outside of the town's newly renovated wellness spa, another one of Fortune Brothers Construction's projects. Paz Spa was going to be opening its doors for the first time this week. Somehow, his brothers had managed to talk him into coming here today for a final walkthrough. That way, they said, he could make sure that the spa was all set to go full speed right out of the starting gate. Reluctantly, because he had never been able to say no to his brothers, he had agreed, even though this wasn't his kind of thing. He was more of a design guy, not a people person. Nevertheless, here he was, trying to get himself to leave the shelter of his vehicle and walk into the spa.

If the spa faltered for some reason, then that might adversely affect their biggest project. The new town hotel—their company's pride and joy—was still on the drawing board. So many factors could get in the way of it becoming a reality.

Again.

There were two different ways of thinking regarding all these new projects he and his brothers had undertaken. The town's older local residents weren't very gung ho when it came to building this new hotel, but the newest segment of the population, the millionaires who had taken up residence within the gated community of Rambling Rose Estates, were definitely all for it. Truthfully, The Shoppes had been built with these people in mind, in the hopes that eventually, with enough prodding, the locals would grudgingly come around. At least they seemed interested in Ashley, Nicole and Megan's farm-to-table restaurant, Provisions, which was set to open within the next few weeks—barring any unforeseen complications.

His brothers were totally convinced that they could get the locals to change their minds, but as for him, well, Dillon had never viewed things in the same sort of positive light that Callum and Steven did. His take on the matter was that the construction company had done all it could here and they should move on to another town.

Preferably one in Florida.

But then, Dillon supposed he had never been as dynamic or optimistic as either Callum or Steven were. Truth be told, Dillon would have been the first to admit that he had always had a far more cautious view of life.

However, he was a Fortune and his brothers made it clear that they were depending on his clear eye to make sure that all systems were "go" before the spa's grand opening.

In other words, they had faith in him.

All things considered, Dillon thought, he would rather have a root canal than face what he was about to endure now.

Well, it wasn't going to get any better or any easier to face with him just sitting here, Dillon thought, finally opening his door.

Swinging out his long legs, he let his boots hit

the ground and he got out of his car. The ache he felt in his shoulders reminded him that he hadn't been exercising lately the way he was accustomed to doing. This project had caused him to let a lot of things in his life slide lately. That was going to have to change.

Closing the car door behind him, he locked it. As he walked toward the entrance of Paz Spa, a line out of an old Tennyson poem he'd once read way back in elementary school suddenly popped up in his head.

"Into the Valley of Death / Rode the six hundred."

Given the challenge of the task ahead, it certainly seemed to capture his mood appropriately enough.

Chapter One

Yup, those were definitely butterflies in her stomach, Hailey Miller decided. They were not only flapping their wings, they were also multiplying like crazy.

Not that she anticipated anything going wrong, the petite spa manager thought, nervously combing her fingers through her long blond hair and pushing the wayward strands away from her face and off to one side. She was just focusing on everything going exactly right for this tour. This was her first time in the role of manager, and she wanted it to be perfect.

That was the reason she had dressed with such

care this morning instead of throwing on a pair of jeans, a comfortable shirt with the spa's logo on it and, like as not, a pair of her favorite boots the way she had done these last few weeks. No, today was special and that was why she had put on a flowing pastel blue dress and a pair of strappy high heels, the ones that flattered her legs. In her opinion, her legs were her best feature and she needed all the help she could get to look her best this morning.

Because this morning she was showing Dillon Fortune around the spa and Dillon Fortune was the man to please, Hailey thought.

The spa, located across the street from the Shoppes, had been his special project and he was the contractor responsible for the spa's newly renovated look. In addition, the man was jaw-droppingly good-looking if the photographs she had seen of him on the internet were any indication. Hailey had a feeling that someone who looked like that was accustomed to being surrounded with beautiful, intelligent women. She definitely didn't want the man to feel as if he was slumming when he conducted his tour through here.

Get a grip, Hailey. He's not going to care what you're wearing, or what you look like. The man's coming here to see what you've done to highlight all the work that was done on the spa.

Just as she pressed her hand against her turbulent stomach, Candace Allen, her new assistant, came hurrying toward her.

"He's here, Hailey," Candace breathlessly announced. "Dillon Fortune!"

Okay, showtime! Hailey took in one last big breath to steady her nerves.

She turned toward her assistant and in that moment saw probably the handsomest man in her near recollection walking in her direction.

Instantly she felt those butterflies of hers revving up for one massive, uncoordinated takeoff.

Even at a distance, she could see that Dillon Fortune looked far more handsome in person than his photographs had made him out to be—and that had been pretty damn near perfect.

Okay, Hailey, you can do this. This is nothing more than a courtesy walk-through for the guy who made all this possible.

So why did part of her suddenly feel as if she were trying to make her way across hot coals?

As Dillon Fortune drew closer, she decided that her fresh wave of nerves had to be due to the look on the man's lean, handsome face. The contractor looked distracted, as if he didn't really want to be here.

Why? Was there something wrong?

Walking up to Dillon and meeting him part of the way, Hailey put out her hand and gave him her widest, most welcoming smile. "Mr. Fortune, I'm Hailey Miller, Paz Spa's manager. I'll be the one giving you a tour of this lovely facility this morning."

Just for a moment, Dillon was caught off guard by the very attractive, animated woman standing before him. For such a petite woman, she had the largest, most expressive blue eyes he had ever seen. He found them almost hypnotic and just for a second, he forgot how much he didn't want to be here.

But then it all came back to him. His intense homesickness, how all of this—the touring, the glad-handing—just felt like such a waste of precious time.

His precious time.

Still, he knew he couldn't be rude. It wasn't this woman's fault that he was halfway across the country from where he wanted to be. And he could see that this perky manager was eager to show the place off to him. A place he felt it prudent not to point out that he was already familiar with, thanks to the fact that he had been the one who had drawn up the initial blueprints and then designed the spa's look from top to bottom.

He offered the petite blonde what he hoped passed for a smile.

"I guess you were the one who wound up drawing the short straw," Dillon told her. Belatedly, he remembered to shake the hand she was still holding out to him.

Hailey could only stare at the contractor. She had no idea what he was saying to her—or why. What short straw? "Excuse me, Mr. Fortune?"

Dillon didn't think he had said anything particularly mysterious. "Well, you obviously have better things to do three days before the spa's grand opening than dropping everything to give one of the people who renovated this place a tour of the exact same area."

Put that way, she didn't know if he resented having her show him around his own work, or if there was something else going on.

"Not really," Hailey answered uncertainly. "We all thought that you might like to see how the ideas all came together to create this rather inviting haven. Everyone here is very eager to have the spa's doors finally open so that our clients can come in and enjoy all the amenities that this place has to offer." If nothing else, she thought, she could be a saleswoman with the best of them.

"As you can see," Hailey continued, gesturing

around the wide-open reception area, "this was all finished with reclaimed wood and other natural materials. It's all extremely pleasing to the eye," she pointed out with pride.

"Now if you'll come this way," Hailey urged as she began to lead the way farther into the spa, "I'll show you some of the inner rooms that will be enjoyed by our clients."

She opened a door that led into a room with a massage table. A mural of a peaceful forest scene on the far wall added to the feeling of tranquility. "We offer various kinds of massage therapy to help our clients relieve some of the stress they've built up during their week. As I'm sure you know, a tense body causes mental stress and may often be responsible for sleeplessness, gastrointestinal distress and headaches, to mention just a few things. The right sort of massage therapy will allow our clients to de-stress and rejuvenate."

Hailey continued talking as she brought Dillon to another room painted in different colors. The main piece of equipment here was the same as in the first room. It all centered around a massage table, except here, there were two tables for the couples looking to reduce their stress levels together.

"I'm sure you'll agree that in this fast-paced life

we all lead, we could certainly use a little revital-
ization, not to mention a small precious island of
time where we can step back from our incredibly
busy lives and just take a deep breath and relax.

"And did you know that a good massage can
also improve your circulation? That means no
more cold hands and feet—if you have them, that
is," she quickly added in case he thought she was
insinuating that this was his problem. "Think how
good that would feel," Hailey added with another
bright smile. "Massage therapy can also help improve your flexibility, strengthen your muscles and
reduce your pain levels by releasing endorphins."

Her hand on his elbow, she gently guided Dillon toward yet another area.

"Now, right over here, Mr. Fortune, is where
we decided to put..."

Hailey continued with what turned out to be a
monologue for another good half hour, opening
various doors and explaining in vivid, glowing
detail what each area was for, be it a sauna, a tan-
ning salon or the aforementioned massage tables.
There were also large rooms where various classes
would be conducted.

"Giving massages is my specialty," she told the
contractor. "I actually began working in the wellness field as a masseuse."

She turned around to see how her one-man audience had received that piece of information. Looking at Dillon, she stopped talking for a moment, wondering if he had heard a single word she had said. He certainly didn't act as if he had. He hadn't made a single comment or said anything at all during the entire tour she had just conducted.

In fact, if she were to hazard a guess, Dillon Fortune was acting as if he would rather be *any-where* else other than here.

Oh, he was being polite, she'd give him that, but the man was also being distant. *Extremely* distant.

And just like that, without any warning, she was five years old all over again. Five years old and desperately trying to engage her father by attempting to show him the new hairstyles she had so painstakingly fashioned for her favorite dolls. He'd been a workaholic who had never had time for her. All she wanted was just a little of his attention, but he was always too busy being success-ful to notice her. Eventually, she gave up trying.

Her father had had that same distant, removed look on his face that was now gracing Dillon Fortune's ruggedly handsome face.

Well, handsome or not, it wasn't good enough as far as she was concerned. Mentally resolved, Hailey decided to give it one last try. She was determined to engage Dillon Fortune on some level so she wouldn't feel as if she were talking to a wall.

Or to a man who just didn't hear her.

"You might have noticed," Hailey started again brightly, "but everything here at the spa has this really good smell about it."

Checking his phone for what felt like the tenth time since he'd arrived, Dillon looked up at his incredibly chipper tour guide. Had she just said something about smelling good, or was that just his imagination?

She was looking at him as if she expected some sort of a reaction from him. "Excuse me?"

"Scent," she repeated. "There's a really good scent here at the spa. That's not by accident," she assured him. "Finding just the right scent is all part of the experience here at Paz. We find that the right scent helps not just soothe our clients but it also invigorates them. We're planning to use some of these scents as part of our aromatherapy massages."

Hailey found herself talking fast now, trying not to lose his attention. To that end, she began showing him all the different bottles of the various scents that the spa had stocked up on.

"Care to take a whiff?" Hailey offered, uncorking one of the bottles. It was jasmine and was her personal favorite.

Dillon shook his head. "No, that's all right."

He was resisting, she thought and took it as a challenge. She was determined to use this latest example of therapy to get through to this man. These scents were meant to soothe a client, to help that person relax, and if there was ever an uptight person who needed to relax, it was definitely Dillon Fortune.

"C'mon," Hailey coaxed, "you can take one whiff, can't you?" She raised the bottle up for Dillon to get a better sense of what was in it. "Go ahead. Try it."

Seeing that she wasn't going to back off until he did as she urged, Dillon said, "Okay, fine, let me smell it." If he didn't breathe in too deeply, he'd be all right, he told himself. And then maybe she'd terminate this tour and let him leave.

Hailey held the open bottle up to his face and Dillon took a deep breath of the scent.

Perhaps a little too deep because the next thing he knew, he was sneezing.

A lot.

Waving Hailey back away from him, he accidentally hit the bottle she was holding up to him.

That in turn sent the entire contents of the bottle flying out and all over his shirt.

And just like that, Dillon found himself utterly drenched in jasmine oil.

Horror stricken by the unfortunate chain of events that had brought about this present dilemma, Hailey could only stare at the drenched man, wide-eyed.

"Oh, my Lord, I am *so* sorry, Mr. Fortune," she cried, embarrassed.

Dillon couldn't comment on her apology at first. Not because he was so angry but because he just couldn't stop sneezing.

Finally, all but wiped out thanks to his sneezing, Dillon could only hold his hand up, silently indicating that she had to stop saying she was sorry.

Damn it, Dillon thought, he smelled like a damn flower garden. Not exactly the scent he was going for, he thought.

He should have known better than to let this woman anywhere near him with that bottle. He wasn't normally prone to allergies, but there were certain scents that could just set him off. He had never investigated the matter or found out which particular scents affected him, but he was aware that there were some that could be devastating to him. So he normally steered clear of all of them.

He realized he should have stuck to that instead of allowing himself to be overwhelmed by a rapid-fire motor mouth.

Dillon waved the petite woman away.

Stunned and embarrassed, as well as somewhat annoyed, she moved back. She was still clutching the bottle. It was obviously empty now, but who knew, maybe whatever traces of the scent that could be left coating the sides of the bottle might still be affecting him.

As if reading his mind, Hailey tossed the bottle into a trash can on the other side of the room.

When she quickly rejoined him, Dillon was still sneezing, although not nearly as violently as before. Hailey realized that he was sneezing because the scent was still around him, thanks to the fact that it had soaked his shirt and was now probably on his chest.

Hailey instantly felt just awful. It was clear that Dillon was suffering.

"Again, I am so sorry," she apologized with feeling. "I didn't know you were allergic to the oils we used. Why didn't you say something?" she wanted to know.

It took Dillon a moment to clear his throat enough to be able to answer her. "Because I'm not allergic to oils," he informed her almost indignantly. And then he was forced to add, "I just have this reaction sometimes when I pass by a department store perfume counter... I mean, not that I go around inhaling perfumes, it's just that sometimes there are these overly zealous sales people spraying perfumes into the air and—"

Dillon had to abruptly stop because he'd started sneezing again.

Hailey saw only one solution to end the man's misery. "You're going to have to take off your shirt," she told him.

Her declaration caught Dillon totally by surprise. He stared at the spa manager, certain that he had misheard her. "Say what?"

"Your shirt. It's soaked," she pointed out in case he had somehow missed that. "Take it off," she instructed. It was half a request, half an order. "I can wash it for you."

The hell she could, he thought. He wasn't about to strip off his shirt.

"No, that's all right," he said as he began backing away. "I can just—"

"What, walk out of here smelling like a flower garden on steroids?" she asked him. There was a skeptical expression on her face. "I don't think so. At the very least, you might wind up attracting bees and being attacked by them. Besides," she said, pausing as Dillon sneezed again, "you're probably not going to stop sneezing until you're separated from that scent. It's clearly all over you, and in your case, apparently a little bit goes a long way. So don't argue with me, Mr. Fortune. Give!" she told Dillon, holding out her hand. "We have a small dedicated laundry area here at the spa. That's how we get our spa robes so clean and fluffy."

Dillon still looked really hesitant about surrendering his shirt.

"That's too much trouble," Dillon told her. "I can just—"

"Oh, I know what the problem is," she told him, realizing why he was hesitating so much—or at least she thought she knew why he wasn't taking his shirt off. After all, he was the spa's contractor. He didn't exactly want to be standing around in his semi-bare glory. The man looked as if he had hard muscles rippling under that shirt of his. Still, being shirtless would undoubtedly prove to be somewhat embarrassing for him. She could understand that.

"Oh?" Despite himself, Dillon's curiosity was aroused by what this woman *thought* she knew.

"Yes," Hailey answered enthusiastically. "You need something to put on," she declared as if she had the inside path to his mind. "Wait right here.

I'm going to go find something for you," she promised, rushing off.

"No, really," Dillon called after her, "you don't have to go to any more trouble."

Especially since she had managed to cause all this trouble just by taking him on a harmless tour of the place to begin with.

But Dillon found he was talking to himself. Hailey Miller, eager beaver par excellence, had rushed off in search of something for him to wear.

Dillon was about to cut his losses and just get out of here before something else went wrong. But his dearly savored escape was quickly aborted when Hailey came hurrying back less than a minute and a half after she had left him standing there dripping.

Instead of a T-shirt with the spa's logo splashed across the front as Dillon would have anticipated, she came back carrying something white and fluffy.

"Here," she announced, holding up what looked like one of the spa robes. "It's the best I could come up with on such short notice—and it does cover everything up." Although, she caught herself thinking, the man did have a really nice set of muscles on him.

Looking at the robe, Dillon suppressed a groan.

Chapter Two

The next second, Dillon's mind did a complete 180 degree turn regarding what he was about to do. Although the bubbly manager was holding out the white robe for him to put on, Dillon decided he wasn't about to put it on.

"No, that's all right," he told Hailey, shaking his head. "I'll just take a pass on putting that on, thanks." He spared one final look at the offered garment, a disapproving expression on his face. "It's not exactly my style." He was rather conservative and the idea of stripping his shirt off in front of a total stranger left him with a bad taste in his mouth.

For a second, Hailey was puzzled. She looked at the robe she was holding out as if she'd never seen it before and reevaluated it.

And then it suddenly dawned on her.

"I didn't mean that you'd have to wear this when you leave," she clarified. "This is just something for you to put on temporarily while I'm getting that overwhelming scent washed out of your shirt. C'mon," she urged, taking a step toward him, holding out the robe again. "The sooner I take the shirt and get started, the sooner you'll get it back."

Dillon took a step back, and then another and another. For her part, Hailey just continued coming toward him. He felt like he was being stalked, while for her part, Hailey felt he was being unduly shy. She was only trying to help.

"No, I said it's okay. Really," he stressed. He didn't know how to make his position any clearer to her.

"But it's *not* okay," Hailey insisted. "I can't have you leaving here like this, with your first impression of the spa being the place where you wound up smelling like a garden full of jasmine on steroids. Consciously or unconsciously, you'll wind up hating the place. And who could blame you?" she told Dillon. "No, you need to take your shirt off so I can wash it," Hailey repeated, more force-fully this time.

He made one last attempt to beg off, but it was becoming very obvious to him that the woman didn't know how to take no for an answer. He opened his mouth to protest again, but before he could say a word, Hailey was already talking.

"Look, Mr. Fortune, I need your shirt," Hailey stated in a friendly but firm tone.

With every step that this persistent petite woman had taken toward him, Dillon had taken an equal step back. But now his back was against the wall—literally—and he had nowhere to go.

The only way he could get her to stop was to raise his voice and tell her to back off, although that really wasn't his style. However, as a last re-sort, he was willing to change his tactics.

And he was just about to, when the slender, vi-vacious spa manager cut him off at the knees. She raised up those big beautiful eyes of hers, aimed them directly at his and then fired the winning salvo.

Hailey said, "Please?"

And just like that, Dillon felt as if he'd been completely disarmed.

With a loud sigh, he conceded that he had lost the battle.

But how was he going to remove the shirt without feeling like a male stripper?

Hailey had always been blessed with the ability to somehow intuit what was going on in a person's mind. She applied that ability to the situation she found herself in at the moment. When she did it, she was able to see exactly why Dillon was still hesitating to give her the shirt.

For some reason, he was embarrassed. Dillon was obviously well built, but apparently he was not one of those men who was comfortable about flaunting it.

"Tell you what," she proposed. "There's no one around here so you can take your shirt off now. I'll even turn around to give you your privacy," Hailey offered, then smiled brightly at him. "You can't really do better than that, Mr. Fortune."

"Oh, I don't know about that," he countered, contemplating whether or not to tell her exactly *how* he could have done better. He could have passed up on this royal pain of a tour altogether, he thought. But saying that out loud sounded cruel to him, so he decided to let it go.

Rather than argue with him, Hailey deliberately turned her back on the man she was determined to impress.

"Any time you're ready," she cheerfully announced, holding the robe out to the side.

Keeping her back to him, Hailey took a single step backward toward the contractor so that the robe would be more accessible for him.

As she did so, because of the angle where he was standing, Hailey realized that she could see his naked upper torso. It was reflected in the side mirror near him and that image was ricocheted back to her via the larger mirror that ran the length of the left wall.

The end result was that she was able to see exactly what he undoubtedly hadn't wanted her to see—Dillon in all of his exceptionally sculpted glory.

Hailey's mouth suddenly went very dry. It became clear to her that she wasn't really able to swallow even if her life depended on it.

Dear Lord, the man was *magnificent*!

It was all Hailey could do not to utter the word out loud.

Belatedly, she realized that she had given herself away because in that first unguarded, unprepared moment, she had sucked in her breath the way someone sitting in the first car of a roller-coaster ride might do just as that car started to take its first plunge down the steep incline.

No matter how prepared she might have thought she was for the sight of this good-looking male, she was not *that* prepared. Seeing all those muscles, all those incredibly hard ridges, even secondhand because she was seeing them all reflected in the mirror, she was totally *un*prepared for the effect that gorgeous body had on her.

Maybe he hadn't heard her, Hailey thought, crossing her fingers.

The next moment, her hopes were dashed. She could see from the raised eyebrows in his reflection that he'd heard her. Moreover, he probably knew that she knew.

Dillon, however, made the decision to carry on the charade and pretend that he *hadn't* heard her sharp intake of breath. It was far safer that way. This way there would be no need to talk about anything.

Ignorance created a welcomed cloak that draped helpfully over everything, he thought as he thrust the shirt in the direction of Hailey's waiting outstretched hand. "Here's my shirt."

"I can tell," she answered, smiling to herself as her fingers closed over the surrendered article. Without turning around—she could tell by the sound that he was just shrugging into the robe she'd given him—Hailey started to hurry off. "I'll get this started. Your shirt will be the only thing in the washing machine so it should be done in no time flat."

It wouldn't be done fast enough for him, Dillon thought.

When Hailey returned to the area several minutes later, Dillon saw that her hands were empty. Still, he couldn't help asking her, "Is the shirt ready yet?"

"The spa's washing machine is the very latest model on the market," Hailey proudly told him. "But it's not *that* fast," she politely pointed out. "Again, I am *so* sorry about all this."

Had he been one of those spiteful people willing to blame everyone else for anything he had to put up with, Dillon would have let her continue beating herself up for dousing his shirt and causing him to practically sneeze his brains out. But to do so wouldn't have been right, or fair and he had too much of a conscience to indulge in that sort of behavior.

"It's not your fault," he told her. "The fault is mine. I wasn't paying close enough attention to what was going on. Like I said, sometimes I have an allergic reaction to certain scents. If I had been paying closer attention to what you were trying to show me, I would have realized that."

Hailey felt his admission opened up a door, leaving her free to talk. Maybe some good could come out of all of this, after all.

"You know, you did look a little preoccupied when I was taking you on that tour," she told him. Actually, he had looked a *lot* preoccupied, but saying that might have sounded as if she were criticizing him, so she left it at her initial statement. Instead, she diplomatically approached the subject she was attempting to broach. "Maybe you could stand to avail yourself of one of the spa treatments we offer here at Paz." Her enthusiasm grew as she continued, "I could personally set up an appointment for you and then—"

Dillon immediately stopped her before she could get carried away. "No. No, thank you. I'm good," he assured her.

The man was good-looking, but he definitely wasn't "good" in the sense he was trying to convey. He needed prodding, she thought.

"Are you sure? Because these treatments can be really helpful, Mr. Fortune. They're designed for the busy executive like yourself. Tell you what," Hailey continued eagerly. "If you feel a little uncomfortable about getting one of our special tailored massages, I would be more than happy to be the one who—"

"Nope, I'm fine," Dillon insisted, cutting her off. "It's all good, really. Thanks, but no thanks," he repeated, leaving the woman absolutely no wiggle room to talk him into anything.

The truth of the matter was he sensed that he could easily be attracted to this woman. The very last thing he needed—or wanted—was for that feeling to escalate. And *that* would be exactly what would happen if she put her hands on his back and torso to work the kinks out of his stiff, sore muscles.

"Okay," Hailey replied compliantly, "if you say so. But I want you to know that if you should decide to change your mind, the offer stands open anytime that you feel the need to try our method of—"

"Thanks, but I won't be changing my mind," Dillon informed her, cutting her off. "Don't worry about it," he stressed rather forcefully. "The only thing I want from you is—"

"Your shirt, yes, I am well aware of that," Hailey said, anticipating what he was about to tell her. She really didn't have to be a mind reader in order to know that.

"Well, yes, that, too," Dillon readily agreed.

"But what I was about to say is that I'd also like you to promise me that you won't mention this incident to my brothers. I doubt if the topic will come up," he added, stating the fact before she had an opportunity to, "but on the outside chance that it might, I'd really rather that they didn't find out about this unfortunate incident."

"Yes, of course. I won't say a word to anyone," Hailey promised him. "Your secret's definitely safe with me, Mr. Fortune."

Dillon laughed despite himself. "Considering everything that has just happened between us, I think you can call me Dillon," he told her.

A smile rose to her lips, so warm in scope that it fascinated him for a couple of moments.

"I'd like that," Hailey told him, then added his name, making what she said sound infinitely more personal. "Dillon."

He caught himself thinking that his name sounded almost lyrical as it came from her lips.

Wow, he was really getting carried away, Dillon upbraided himself. At best this was just a business meeting that had gone wrong, nothing more. Besides, as Hailey had already pointed out, his mind had been elsewhere, not here.

"Would your brothers really give you a hard time if they knew about this?" she asked, curious.

Hailey immediately backtracked when she saw Dillon's brow go up. She didn't want him getting the wrong idea. "Not that I'd ever mention any of this," she quickly added, trying her best to reassure him. "Because I'd never say a word. To anyone," she emphasized once again. "Really," Hailey stressed. "I just asked you that because I was curious about what it was like, having all those siblings around. People who you know you can always lean on, no matter what." That sounded like heaven to her. "How many siblings do you have again?" she asked, cocking her head.

He was doing his best not to get distracted again. There was something about this woman that tended to do that to him. Anyway, why would she want to know that? he couldn't help wondering.

"I have seven," he finally answered. He kept the fact that some were half siblings to himself. Continuing to remain cautious, Dillon watched the woman's face as he asked, "Why?"

Hailey shrugged. "No reason. I was just thinking that it had to be nice, having that many siblings around. You always have someone to talk to, someone to turn to for advice. I just have one sister," she told him. "And I have to admit that I always thought it would have been really great to come from a large family."

Dillon shrugged, thinking of the people who comprised his family and of some of the incidents that had occurred while he was growing up.

"It has its moments, I suppose," he admitted somewhat reluctantly.

"Like what?" she asked, her tone encouraging him to elaborate.

Damn, it was happening again. He was getting distracted. Why did this woman have that effect on him? She seemed so guileless…

He had to snap out of it! He really needed to be on his way.

Dillon glanced at his watch again, then at her. "Could you check to see if my shirt's ready yet?"

The man looked as if he were ready to jump out of his skin at any second, Hailey observed. She wondered if she'd said something to set him off.

His question had her snapping to attention. "Oh, right. Sorry, I guess I forgot about that," she confessed. "But you obviously didn't," she added with a smile. She could feel herself growing nervous again. "How could you, standing there in that robe?" she asked. "I didn't mean to go on like that," she apologized for what felt like the dozenth time since he had arrived at the spa. "I'll go right now and see if it's ready." She hurried off.

It wouldn't be ready, he thought. Not unless the

shirt somehow "knew" it had to dry itself after it had finished washing.

He glanced at his watch again. How much longer was he going to have to hang around this place waiting for his shirt to dry?

Not that being with this woman was any sort of actual hardship, he amended in all honesty. Under any other set of circumstances, he might have even welcomed the excuse.

But right now, he felt like a total idiot and standing around in this long fluffy robe just seemed to intensify that reaction.

It also upped the chances of someone coming in and seeing him looking like this.

He *really* wanted to get out of here.

Now.

Chapter Three

A while later, the dryer Hailey had put Dillon's newly washed shirt into was still running.

To check, Hailey pressed the pause button on the oversized machine and it tumbled to a noisy halt.

Opening the door, she fished out Dillon's shirt, ran her hand over the material and frowned. It still felt a bit damp. Not dripping, she conceded, but definitely damp. If given a choice, she knew that she wouldn't have wanted to put it on. The damp material would feel clammy against her skin.

Against *his* skin, Hailey corrected herself.

She was about to put the shirt back into the

dryer when she heard Dillon's deep voice coming from directly behind her.

"Is it ready yet?"

Surprised, she turned around. He'd followed her. She wouldn't have thought that he would. The laundry room wasn't all that hard to find, but coming here necessitated walking out into the hallway wearing that long, flowing fluffy robe—and being *seen* wearing it, something she'd gotten the very strong impression that he wanted to avoid.

The man *really* had to be anxious to get out of here, she thought.

Even so, Hailey felt she had to be honest with him. "No, not really." She looked down at the shirt as she spoke, and when her eyes raised, she noticed Dillon had crossed the floor and was now standing right beside her.

For some reason, being alone in the room with Dillon and envisioning him naked from the waist up beneath the spa robe made the hairs along her arms all stand up, almost at attention.

You're not being very professional, Hailey. You've had undraped men on your massage table before and it's never affected you.

Still, the appealing vision of Dillon Fortune that had popped up was a difficult one to banish from her brain.

"Let me see it," Dillon was saying. He put his hand out expectantly, waiting for his shirt.

"Okay." Hailey held the blue silk shirt out to him. "Go ahead, touch it," she coaxed.

The moment the words were out of her mouth, she realized how they must have sounded to him. They sounded like an invitation. Embarrassed, she cleared her throat. "I mean, you can see that it's still pretty damp," she told Dillon, avoiding his eyes. "If you give it a few more minutes—"

"That's all right," Dillon said, overriding the woman's protest. At this point, in order to be on his way, Dillon would have worn the shirt even if it were completely sopping wet.

His urge to bolt was so strong that he allowed the robe to drop off his shoulders. It fell to the floor as he slipped on his shirt. He was so intent on putting it on, he didn't see the startled look, immediately followed by an appreciative one, passing over Hailey's face. But she was very aware of it as she caught her reflection in the dryer door.

Damn, she'd already seen the man's sculpted torso, but seeing its reflection completely paled to viewing the man up close and personal like this. Hailey felt a wave of intense heat pass over her and it was all she could do to keep her knees from buckling.

How was this man walking around unattached and without legions of starry-eyed, eager women following him around, desperate for his attention? It made no sense to her.

Breathe, Hailey, breathe. He isn't interested in you that way. His desire to make a hasty exit makes that perfectly clear. Don't complicate matters by drooling on him.

Meanwhile, Dillon was still getting dressed. It was a little tricky, pushing his arms into the damp sleeves, but it was amazing what a man could do when pressured by a sense of urgency.

"The main thing," he told her, "is that that smell is gone."

As if to test his statement, Hailey leaned in toward his chest and took a deep breath. She wrinkled her nose a little.

"Well, actually, there's still a trace of it left," she told him. Wait. What was she doing, stepping so close to him and smelling him? Had she lost all sense of professionalism?

After a moment's hesitation, Dillon leaned back. "I—" He stopped, then started again, regaining his thoughts. With her so close, it wasn't easy. "It's good enough," he finally declared. "As long as it doesn't attract a swarm of bees, I'm ahead of the game."

"But if you just give it a few more minutes, Mr. Fortune…" she tactfully protested. In light of his obvious anxiousness to flee, she had reverted back to his surname, feeling that to call him *Dillon* was far too familiar right now.

"I'm already late for…something," Dillon said evasively.

That would explain his constantly looking at his watch and his phone while she had been taking him on the tour, she thought. The pang that went through her was involuntary. Did he have a hot date waiting for him? Or maybe he was going to be meeting up with his next conquest?

It was none of her business, Hailey silently told herself. Whoever it was, the person was obviously enough to distract him.

Hailey bent over to pick up the fallen robe and slung it over her arm as he finished buttoning his still damp shirt. It seemed to cling to every ridge, every ripple, she couldn't help noticing.

Keeping her face forward, Hailey fell into place beside him as Dillon started walking toward the front exit.

"Will we be seeing you at the grand opening?" she asked.

Focused on making his retreat, as well as on what time it was, Dillon hadn't heard her. But by the look he saw on her face, the woman was obviously waiting for some sort of response from him.

"What?" he asked, still walking as he tucked his shirt into his slacks.

"The grand opening, it's in a few days," Hailey prompted. "Will we be seeing you there?"

"Oh. Right. Yes, of course. Wouldn't miss it," he assured her a second before he made good his escape.

"I don't know about that," Hailey murmured under her breath as she watched him hurrying down the front steps. "You seemed to have missed the tour, even though you were physically here for it."

With a sigh, Hailey turned away from the spa's large double-glass doors.

"So? How did it go?" Candace asked.

Hailey's assistant seemed to materialize directly behind her the moment that the contractor had walked out of the building.

"It went," was all that Hailey allowed herself to say.

Candace frowned. "Well, that doesn't sound very good."

Hailey tactfully walked back her initial assessment. "It could have gone better," she amended. "I got the impression that Mr. Fortune's mind was elsewhere during most of the tour."

"His mind was probably on his next project," the young woman guessed.

Or his next conquest by the looks of it, Hailey thought. She had seen men preoccupied with the women in their lives, or the women they were about to have in their lives. Dillon had all the signs.

But, for the sake of the spa and things moving forward on that front, Hailey decided to agree with her assistant. "You're probably right. He was undoubtedly thinking about his next project. I guess I'm being just a little bit edgy."

Still, despite her pep talk to herself to the contrary, Hailey couldn't help being curious about who the person on the other end of Dillon Fortune's phone had been. Whoever it was was wreaking havoc in what otherwise seemed like Dillon Fortune's orderly world.

To her way of thinking, the butterflies that Hailey had experienced at the beginning of the week while she had waited to give the handsome contractor a tour of the spa were just a dry run for what she assumed she would be experiencing today, at the spa's official grand opening ceremony.

But oddly enough, she turned out to be wrong. To Hailey's surprise, when the big day came, she was completely calm.

Hailey had spent the days between then and now overseeing every single detail involved in the grand opening, then going over them twice, from the festive decorations to the extensive array of catered food. She'd even easily handled the last-minute shipments of some equipment. Mercifully, nothing rattled her.

She survived it all and when the big day finally did arrive, she was ready hours ahead of time. To her relief, the butterflies in her stomach seemed to remain subdued.

One of the first people to arrive to the festivities was Ellie Fortune Hernandez, Rambling Rose's mayor and Steven Fortune's recent blushing bride. As expected, Steven was at her side.

The mayor was scheduled to make an appropriate speech about how the spa was one of the projects that were already revitalizing the town and how she anticipated that this feeling would be on the upswing in the weeks to come, thanks to other projects that were in the works.

Waiting for the official ribbon-cutting ceremony to take place, everyone meandered around the front of the spa, availing themselves of the refreshments that were set up on tables before the front doors. Hailey was there to play hostess to the gathering crowd.

The slender dark-haired mayor and her six-foot-tall husband were still practically newlyweds. The striking couple definitely looked the part. Anyone looking at them could see that they still had that newlywed glow about them, although Hailey was willing to bet part of that glow was due to the fact that Ellie Hernandez was also pregnant. Her condition was just now beginning to show and no matter what the young mayor talked about, she seemed to be literally beaming.

Hailey found that she was both very happy for Ellie as well as just a little bit envious of the woman. Hailey could only imagine what it had to be like to be that in love with someone and to be that loved in return. In Hailey's estimation, anticipating the birth of a baby only added to that perfect scenario, increasing happiness by a hundredfold.

She sincerely doubted that it would ever happen for her.

Don't bite off more than you can chew, Hailey.

Just as she was about to say something to Ellie, the mayor beat her to it. Ellie came up to her, gestured about the immediate area and said, "So I see congratulations are in order."

Hailey's eyes dipped down to the mayor's waist. It was still very trim looking, but Hailey could see that it was just beginning to widen in order to accommodate its new little boarder.

"I hear the same can be said to you and your husband, Madam Mayor," Hailey responded, looking over Ellie's shoulder and catching a glimpse of Steven who was talking to someone.

Ellie offered her a serene smile, the kind that was so commonly seen gracing the faces of expectant mothers.

"Thank you," Ellie responded, her eyes shining. The next moment, the mayor's husband came up to join them. He rested his hand protectively on Ellie's shoulder.

"Don't you think you should be sitting down?" he tactfully asked her.

"I feel fine," Ellie assured him. "Really." Looking at Hailey, the mayor decided she needed to explain her husband's display of concern. He wasn't just being a typical nervous husband. "I had a touch of morning sickness earlier, but it's gone now. Really," she repeated, underscoring the word for her husband's benefit. "I'm not a fragile little flower, ready to wilt at the slightest provocation," Ellie insisted. "I never have been."

"Well, between you and me, Ms. Miller, my wife wouldn't say a word even if she was at death's door," Steven confided to Hailey.

Ellie laughed, waving away her husband's obvious concern.

"Luckily, I'm not," she insisted. "I—" She pulled up short as she pointed at two men who'd just arrived. "Steven, look. Aren't those your cousins?" she asked.

Hailey and the mayor's husband both turned to see who the mayor was referring to. The two men who had just walked up the spa's front steps definitely bore a striking resemblance to not only Steven but to several other Fortunes, as well.

But while the two men looked vaguely familiar to Hailey, Steven recognized the duo almost immediately.

"You're right," he agreed. "That's Adam and Kane Fortune. They're my Uncle Gary's two oldest sons," he said for Hailey's benefit since he knew she wasn't as up on the Fortune family tree as he and his wife were.

"Are they in the construction business, too?" Hailey asked, making what seemed like a logical assumption to her.

Steven laughed under his breath. "I think they probably think they are."

Hailey was trying to follow what Steven was saying. "So they're *not* part of your construction company?" she asked the mayor's husband.

She knew that Steven as well as Callum were both part of the same company that Dillon was part of. All of them had helped make the spa and several other new projects in Rambling Rose a reality in the last few months. The Fortune brothers were responsible for breathing life into the fading town.

"No," Steven said with feeling. "They're most definitely *not* part of the company. They're recently in from New York, but I think they're here to get the lay of the land and they either plan to eventually ask to join up with our company, or to form one of their own. To be honest," he confessed, "it's not exactly clear to any of us yet." And by *us*, Hailey knew he was referring to Callum, Dillon and himself.

The next second, Adam and Kane came up to join them.

"Hey, you guys did a great job here," Adam announced in a loud voice. "Too bad we didn't arrive here sooner so we could have gotten in on the ground floor with all this."

"There'll be more projects," Steven answered vaguely. "Right, Dillon?" he asked, looking over his cousin's shoulder toward his brother.

The latter had just arrived and was silently taking all this in.

Ellie turned around to face her brother-in-law.

"When did you get here? I don't remember seeing you when we got here a few minutes ago."

"That's because I just arrived," Dillon answered. For some reason, he felt it prudent to avoid Hailey's eyes. Instead, he nodded at his two cousins. "Kane. Adam."

"They were just saying how much they regret not having arrived in Rambling Rose sooner, that way they would have been here to help work on the various construction projects that are either going up or being renovated. Seems that they think this is a good place to invest in and build up," Steven told his brother pointedly.

Ellie picked up on her husband's tone and looked from him to his brother. "Am I missing something here, boys?"

Steven smiled. "Dillon's the family Cassandra," he explained. He continued despite the frown on Dillon's face. "You know, the woman in Greek mythology who always foresaw all the bad things that were going to happen."

"I didn't say something bad was going to happen," Dillon insisted. "I just don't wear the same rose-colored glasses that you and Callum do," he said flatly.

Hailey was trying to follow what was being

said. "You didn't want to renovate this spa?" she asked him.

Rather than attempt to deny the statement, Dillon tried to explain his thinking. "I just didn't think the town was ready for it. The bottom line was profit and I just didn't think that there was going to be that much profit to be made here, not the way my brothers did," he explained.

"Let me put it this way," Steven responded. "Callum and I see the glass half full and getting fuller by the minute, while Dillon here—" he glanced at his brother with an affectionate smile "—well, his glass is always half empty. Not only that, but the glass is leaking, as well. Am I right, Dillon?"

Dillon didn't believe in washing dirty laundry in public. And even if he did, this wasn't the time to do that or to argue, not at an important grand opening ceremony and definitely not in front of his cousins and a stranger, even a very attractive, sexy one. He decided to let the topic go. Any actual discussions he needed to undertake would be conducted with his brothers in private.

Smiling at his brother, Dillon inclined his head. "Close enough, brother," he said to Steven.

Chapter Four

Steven Fortune inclined his head in close to his wife's ear and whispered, "Looks like it's time, Madam Mayor." When Ellie turned her head to look up at him, he asked, "Are you ready, or do you need a little more time? I can stall if you'd like." Taking nothing for granted, Steven was concerned that, even now, his wife might be battling another wave of morning sickness.

Her husband's thoughtfulness touched her each and every time he displayed it. Once again, Ellie thought how very lucky she was that the two of them had found one another. When she thought of the odds against that happening, against her finding her soul mate, especially when she was already carrying another man's child, Ellie was nothing if not humbled.

Grateful, Ellie squeezed her husband's hand. "I'm fine," she told him.

Taking her at her word, Steven moved over toward Dillon and gave his brother a thumbs-up sign.

"Looks like it's time," he told his brother in a quiet voice.

Watching them interact, Dillon found himself envying their closeness, and wishing he could find someone to love him who loved him back the way Steven had.

Ordinarily, Dillon didn't welcome being in the spotlight. However, Ellie would be the one with all eyes on her and he knew his brother's new wife thrived on the favorable attention.

"Everyone," Dillon said, raising his voice as he addressed the people in front of the wellness spa. "If I could have your attention for a moment, please," he began.

Slowly, more and more people turned to look in Dillon Fortune's direction, their conversations halting until relative silence reigned.

"I want to welcome all of you here today and thank you for coming," Dillon said, addressing the gathering. With that, he turned the proceedings over to the town's mayor. "Madam Mayor, they're all yours," Dillon told her.

All eyes turned toward Ellie, waiting for her to cut the white ribbon and officially open up the spa to make it become a part of the townspeople's lives.

"I'm not going to bore you with a long, fancy speech or a lot of rhetoric," Ellie began warmly. "We all know why we're here."

"Yeah, for the refreshments," someone in the back of the crowd called out.

Laughter rippled through the crowd.

"Exactly," Ellie agreed. "Refreshments for our bodies as well as for our souls, which is exactly what this spa with all its new techniques and amenities promises to deliver," the mayor told her constituents. "Paz Spa brings what all of us would agree is a much needed shot in the arm to the residents of Rambling Rose. I for one can't thank the Fortune family enough for having traveled here and bringing their ideas and their revitalizing energy to our heretofore sleepy little town. Though in the beginning, some of us weren't quite convinced about the merits of this undertaking, you," she said, pausing to smile at her husband and at Dillon, "have shown us the error of our thinking. Believe me when I tell you that you have earned our undying gratitude many times over.

"In the famous words of Humphrey Bogart at

the end of the classic film *Casablanca*, 'I think this is the beginning of a beautiful friendship.' And I can say that we are all looking forward to watching that *friendship* unfold and thrive.

"So now, without any further ado," Ellie declared, taking hold of the over-sized scissors that Dillon had handed to her, "let me cut this ribbon and declare Paz Spa officially open for business!"

With that, holding onto the two large halves of the scissors, one in each hand, the young mayor cut through the fabric. The two severed white halves of ribbon fluttered to the floor amid enthusiastic cheers.

Steven put his arm around Ellie's shoulders as he pressed a kiss to her temple. "Well done, Madam Mayor," he told her with a pleased laugh.

"Actually, holding onto those two ends and getting them to cut through the ribbon isn't all that challenging," Ellie cracked.

"Well, you pulled it off with grace, the way everyone knew you would." Hailey knew that some women had a tough time coordinating the demands of their jobs with pregnancy. But Ellie seemed to sail right through things, unaffected.

"I wasn't worried," Ellie said, glancing over her shoulder toward her husband. And then her dark eyes twinkled. "I had a backup waiting in the wings."

"Everyone, please, there's a lot of food waiting for you to do justice to it. So eat, drink and—well, you all know the rest of that saying. Now go do it!" Hailey instructed, waving the crowded gathering to move into the spa's reception area where a buffet had been set up.

There were all sorts of sandwiches as well as several kinds of tortillas to choose from. Alongside that were different cuts of fried chicken. They were sitting next to french fries, pizza slices and so many different kinds of pastries, Dillon lost count when he'd tried to catalog them. There were also a selection of salads, smoothies and fresh fruit for the dedicated purists.

When he'd instructed the spa's manager to spare no expense for this celebration, he hadn't thought that much of his words, but she had obviously taken them to heart.

Coming up to Hailey, Dillon felt that he had to tell her what he thought of the tempting array.

"You certainly do know how to put on an inviting spread."

Hailey turned toward the sound of the deep male voice and smiled warmly up at Dillon. She appreciated him telling her that.

"Thank you, I'm glad you approve. I wasn't sure exactly what you had in mind," she confessed, "so

I figured that if I got a little of everything, I'd wind up covering it."

"Yes, I noticed," he said with a laugh. "If we get locked in here for a week for some reason, we certainly wouldn't starve," Dillon commented. "By the way, I didn't see a bill for all this." He felt he had to bring that up because he didn't want her getting stuck footing the bill for this celebration. From what he gathered, she wasn't being paid enough for that.

"That's because I haven't forward it to you yet," Hailey told him.

She had been so completely immersed in all the preparations there'd been no time to pull the tab together. But it was nice of him to make that point.

"Well, just make sure you do," Dillon told her. He looked around the huge salon again with all the people milling around, enjoying themselves. "Everything really looks great, Hailey," he repeated with feeling, as well as an element of approval.

Hailey could feel that same warm sensation spread out all through her again. "Thank you, Mr. Fortune."

Dillon looked surprised that she had used his surname. "I thought we decided you were going to call me by my given name," he reminded her.

"Sorry, I forgot." She hadn't, but by the time he'd left the spa last time, wearing his not-quite-dry shirt and hurrying off to his car, Hailey felt that their relationship had reverted back to its previous formal standing.

"Well, call me Dillon," he instructed.

The next moment, someone else was calling out his name. It turned out to be one of his cousins and Hailey got the impression that he didn't look all that anxious to respond.

"I guess this is a case of careful what you wish for," she said, taking a chance that her observation wouldn't sound too familiar.

Rather than take offense, Dillon laughed softly to himself.

"You can sure say that again." He sighed. He could see that his cousin was *not* going away. "I'd better go see what Adam wants."

Judging by the expression on his face, Hailey had a feeling that he already knew exactly what his cousin wanted to see him about. Adam and Kane Fortune had made no secret of the fact that they wanted to get into the "family" business, not because they harbored any desires to expand Rambling Rose commercially—or to expand any other town that way for that matter. What the cousins seemed to want to be part of were the resulting profits that would be coming down the pike.

Very soon, they hoped.

Hailey watched as Dillon made his way over to his cousin Adam. One minute the contractor had been smiling at her, the next he was withdrawing, as if folding his tent and all but disappearing into the night.

Not again, she thought.

She honestly didn't know what to make of the man, but she did know that she really wanted the opportunity to be able to get to know him better so she could make an intelligent decision about him. That way she could see if they had anything in common outside of those sparks she'd felt the other day, as well as today. Some sparks fizzled while others, if fanned, could turn into a roaring fire.

But first, of course, she needed to get the man to stand still in one place long enough for her to make up her mind about him.

And this was not the right time.

Right now, she needed to mingle and promote the spa's many services. This seemed like the perfect opportunity, while everyone was in a festive, receptive mood and the spa was brand new and at its most appealing.

In her new mindset, the first person Hailey came across was Ellie Hernandez who, for once, wasn't surrounded by a gaggle of people. And the mayor's husband seemed to be otherwise occupied, as well.

She had the woman all to herself.

"That was a very nice opening speech, Madam Mayor," Hailey said, coming closer to the young woman.

"Thank you. It was impromptu," Ellie confessed to Hailey.

"It didn't sound as if it was," Hailey told the woman in all honesty.

"Normally I prepare in advance," she explained and then confided, "but I'm afraid this pregnancy is taking a toll on me and wearing me down more than I'd like to admit."

"Really?" Hailey asked, her interest really piqued now. "Well, lucky for you, I just might have the answer for that." Nothing gave her more pleasure than helping someone *and* advancing the spa's clientele.

"The answer?" the mayor questioned. "I don't think I understand."

Hailey smiled. "Well, Paz Spa offers prenatal massages. They're specially tailored to the particular difficulties that the mother-to-be—meaning you—might be experiencing. These sessions are guaranteed to make a brand new, relaxed woman out of you instead of having you feel as if you were hauling around increasingly heavier, not to mention exceedingly uncooperative, large cargo."

"Right now, making a new woman out of me

sounds like heaven," Ellie told her with a deep appreciative sigh. "Where do I sign up?" she asked enthusiastically.

Was she kidding, Hailey wondered. Or didn't she know? "For you, Madam Mayor—and especially seeing that you have this marital connection to the contractor—all the sessions would be free."

Ellie looked surprised as she shook her head, turning down the offer.

"Nonsense, absolutely not. I'm not going to take advantage of my so-called *connection* to the Fortune family. Besides, how is the spa going to make any money if I do something like that?" the mayor wanted to know.

"Well, I am planning to have at least a few more clients than just you," Hailey said with a laugh. "Not to mention that if you enjoy your sessions and, more importantly, find that they really help you, maybe you can pass the word along. You know, tell your friends. Word-of-mouth is a very good way to advertise the spa," Hailey told her.

"Oh, I'm sure the sessions will help and I can definitely spread the word about the spa," the woman agreed.

Hailey's eyes sparkled as she put out her hand to the mayor. "Wonderful. In that case, I believe we have ourselves a deal," she said, enthusiastically shaking the woman's hand.

Just then, out of the corner of her eye, Hailey saw Dillon go by. He was talking to his other cousin now. For a second, Hailey's attention shifted to the contractor and she temporarily lost her train of thought.

The man did have a way of getting to her, even when she wasn't expecting it, Hailey thought ruefully. She was going to have to watch that.

When she looked back at Ellie, the woman had an amused expression on her face.

"Something on your mind, Hailey?"

For a second, Hailey debated asking the question and then she decided, why not? She really didn't have anything to lose and maybe, just maybe, there might be something to be gained.

"Well," Hailey began cautiously in a lowered voice, "as a matter of fact, since you are married to Steven Fortune…"

"Yes?" Ellie asked, her tone nothing if not encouraging.

Hailey gathered her courage to her and forced herself to push on. Friendly though she was, this wasn't easy for her.

"I thought that you might know what his brother's status is."

"I'm sure I do," Ellie agreed. "Which brother is it?"
Idiot. Her husband's got more than one brother.

"Dillon. The contractor who renovated this spa," she qualified, making it sound as if it was the all-important connection rather than her own reaction to the man.

"Well, Dillon's unattached," Ellie told her. "But…" Her voice trailed off, sounding uncertain.

Although distant alarms went off in Hailey's head, for some reason the mayor's words only aroused Hailey's curiosity even more. "But what?"

"To be honest," Ellie confessed, "I don't know if Dillon's really in the market for anyone."

That was an odd way to put it, Hailey thought. "Do you mean at the moment, or ever?"

Ellie glanced toward her brother-in-law and then sighed. That in itself wound up raising far more questions than it could possibly answer.

"I really don't think I should be the one to answer that, Hailey," the mayor admitted. "I'm afraid that you're going to have to ask Dillon that question." And then Ellie squeezed her hand. "Now, if you'll excuse me, I'm afraid that I'm required to mingle with the good citizens of Rambling Rose or they won't feel as if they've gotten their full nickel's worth."

Hailey laughed as she stepped back, clearing a

path for the mayor. "I had no idea you were charging admission to this."

Ellie smiled in response. "If I did, it would be a great deal more than just a nickel," she told Hailey, winking at her.

Left alone, Hailey caught herself intrigued by and thinking about what Ellie had just told her.

Was what the mayor said true? *Was* there some reason that Dillon Fortune had withdrawn from the dating field? But if that was the case, why had he kept checking his phone so often the other day when she'd been trying to give him a tour of the place? A man who wasn't interested in interacting with potential dating candidates didn't "half" dabble in the field. He was either in or he was out.

And if he was "in," well then, the game was on, wasn't it? And that in turn meant that she was going to have to buckle down and give this her all.

Hailey made up her mind.

She was well aware that she might regret this path she was contemplating taking, but she still wanted to see where it would lead her.

It was settled.

She was definitely in.

Chapter Five

Hours later, after the spa had emptied out and all the well-wishers had gone home, Hailey joined some of the members of her staff to clean up the party area. She wasn't the kind of boss who delegated tasks and then just stood back while they were done. She firmly believed in working alongside her people. And right now, the wellness spa needed to be ready for business bright and early the following morning.

Her problem, Hailey thought as she was working next to her assistant and one of the other instructors, was that she had always allowed her heart to rule her head. This kind of thinking, she readily admitted, left her open to new experiences, allowed her to easily make new friends and, in some cases, find new loves.

As far as that last part went, Hailey was willing to acknowledge that thinking this way had also gotten her into trouble on more than one occasion. If she were being honest, she would be forced to admit that she'd had a series of what her parents had once told her they considered *unsuitable* boyfriends.

But, to her credit, Hailey thought, she had bounced back each and every time. Thanks to her positive frame of mind, she had remained relatively unscarred and more than willing to take yet another plunge into the swirling, turbulent waters of romantic encounters.

And that in turn was all thanks to her personal philosophy. Hailey made no secret of the fact that she firmly believed that life was too short to hang back warily regarding the waters that were up ahead, too afraid to test them.

Her way of looking at things was all because of Janelle.

Sweet and funny, Janelle Walters had been her best friend all throughout elementary school and high school. She and Janelle had been completely inseparable during all those years, sharing secrets, making plans for the future. They were both determined to do great things once they graduated from school and, acting as each other's cheering squad, they always encouraged each other.

The world, they both felt, was at their feet, just waiting for them to dive right into it.

Of the two of them, Janelle had always been the bolder one, the one who didn't back away no matter how great the challenge confronting her. On the rare occasions that Hailey hesitated, Janelle would always be there to urge her along, to tell her that the only thing she had to be afraid of was *not* trying.

Hailey had worshipped her. In Hailey's eyes, Janelle had seemed utterly invincible, a bright shining light in a sometimes darker world, who was always willing to do anything, try anything.

It seemed to Hailey that there wasn't *anything* that Janelle couldn't do.

And then her friend got sick.

Really sick.

Janelle merely shrugged it off, saying it was nothing, that she just needed to eat better, or take some vitamins. No big deal. But eventually, even Janelle couldn't ignore her weakening state.

Alarmed, Janelle's mother finally all but dragged her friend to see a doctor. And then another doctor. And another. They all said the same terrible words that caused the light to go out for Hailey.

Pancreatic cancer.

When she first heard the diagnosis, Hailey had felt completely devastated. But Janelle, her incredible, ever upbeat friend, refused to accept the diagnosis, refused to give up or surrender to the ever-encroaching disease that was, for all intents and purposes, a death sentence. Instead, Janelle fought the good fight, behaving as if "forever" was still in front of both of them and that she would triumph over this so-called "obstacle" and move on.

Right up until the end.

And when the end finally came, just before Janelle finally lost her brave fight, her friend had turned to her and whispered, "Now you have to live for both of us. Promise me you'll live for both of us." Weak, she had tried to tighten her fingers around Hailey's and implored, "Promise me."

Hailey vividly recalled that she could hardly speak because of all the tears that had filled her throat, but somehow, she managed to make the promise to her dearest friend.

Janelle died several hours later. There had actually been a smile on her friend's face as she passed from one world to the next.

Hailey had been utterly inconsolable at first, grieving over the life that had been so cruelly cut short. But then, at her lowest point, she could have sworn she heard Janelle's voice whispering to her, reminding her of her promise.

Drying her eyes, Hailey resolved to honor her promise to her best friend, to live for both of them. Committed, she never looked back.

Janelle was also the reason why Hailey was so totally dedicated to furthering the wellness spa's agenda. She felt it was her own small way of honoring Janelle's memory.

And, of course, Janelle was also the reason why she was so determined to live life to the fullest. She had learned firsthand that life could be incredibly fleeting. For that reason, it needed to be enjoyed to the fullest before it suddenly disappeared.

And that was why she knew she had made the right decision today. She had to seek out Dillon Fortune and see if there was something there.

Hailey didn't realize it then, but spending time cleaning up the discarded plates and cups turned out to be the last peaceful moments she would spend. The very next day, as soon as the spa's doors were opened, the pace was keenly ramped up to almost an insane level.

It seemed as if everyone who had attended the opening ceremony was now eager to find out just what the wellness spa had to offer in the way of improving their lives.

Because of that, business was immediately robust. It remained that way, not just for a few hours but for the remainder of the day, and it had all the signs of continuing at this stride without letting up.

Hailey was determined to do her part to make it continue. She was everywhere at once, answering questions, conducting a variety of demonstration sessions, welcoming new clients. She kept this pace up from the moment the doors opened until they closed again for the night that evening.

Two days later, happily exhausted, Hailey knew a lot of people would have said that it was too soon to think of the wellness spa as a success. The situation could change drastically once the spa's novelty had worn off. But Hailey had never been someone to wallow in sobering thoughts, nor was she someone who prudently restrained and tempered her enthusiasm.

As a result, her enthusiasm knew absolutely no bounds.

So anyone within close proximity could see that she was thrilled by this onslaught of clients and prospective clients crowding into the various classes.

By the fourth day, as she continued taking all this in, Hailey didn't even bother to attempt to hide her wide smile. As if it had a life of its own, the smile spread out from ear to ear.

Silently congratulating herself on her part on

this achievement, she felt as if it looked like the wellness spa was a rip-roaring success.

We did it again, Janelle. We're a success. And I couldn't have done it without you!

Ever alert, Hailey had taken note of the fact that over the last few days several members of the Fortune family had dropped by to check things out. They had all come away looking as if they were well pleased.

At the last minute, just before the spa had had its official grand opening, Hailey had felt inspired and had added an additional class to the roster. A yoga class specifically designed for mothers and their babies, although an asterisk to the left of the listing in the brochure told any interested parties that fathers were welcome to the class, as well.

When the first day for the class arrived, Hailey was delighted that one of the enrollees was Callum Fortune's new wife, Becky. A former widow and a nurse at the new pediatric center, Becky was the mother of very lively one-year-old twin girls, Luna and Sasha. She brought them with her to class. The girls gave the impression of barely contained little rockets who were ready to go off at any second.

The slim dark-haired nurse was holding her own at the moment, but it looked as if that situation was touch and go and liable to change at any given moment.

Although she had been the one to come up with the class in the first place, Hailey wasn't scheduled to teach it herself. However she had decided to hang around the class in case she was needed to offer help or some advice. Seeing Becky and her girls, Hailey was glad that she made this decision.

Taking leave of the woman she had just been talking to, Hailey made her way over toward the slightly frazzled-looking young woman who appeared to be struggling mightily to hold onto her daughters and keep them both in the same area.

"Hi," Hailey said brightly, greeting Callum's wife. She ran her hand over Sasha's—or was it Luna's—hair. "Looks like you've really got your hands full, Becky." Hailey smiled at the two upturned faces that were presently regarding her with unbridled curiosity. "If you don't mind my saying so, you're pretty brave, taking on this class by yourself with both your little girls at the same time."

"Oh, I'm not alone," Becky told her as one of the twins attempted to tug away from her. Becky managed to hold onto her—for now. "At least, I won't be for long." She suppressed a rather deep sigh. "Callum said he was coming to lend not just his support but his two hands, as well." Her smile wasn't forced, but it did seem just a wee bit weak around the edges as she held the potential runaway closer to her body. "I don't think I can manage this all by myself, at least not the first few times," she confided. "They just have too much energy!"

Because of all the various interactions that she had experienced these last couple of weeks, Hailey was beginning to feel as if she were actually part of the family, even though her only real connection to the Fortunes was this wellness spa that the brothers had built. But Hailey had always had the ability to make friends easily and the men's spouses had been quick to open up to her. They'd talked to her as if she were one of them almost from the start, and Hailey had responded in kind, welcoming the bonding experience.

"Tell you what," Hailey suggested, slipping her fingers around one of the twins' small hands. "Why don't I just hang around a bit and help out until your husband arrives with his own set of very capable hands?"

Although Becky looked grateful at the offer, she felt it only right to respond with a protest at first. "I wouldn't feel right about taking you away from all your other commitments."

"Oh, you're not," Hailey was quick to assure the woman. She wasn't just being polite. She genuinely liked the nurse and wanted to do whatever she could to allow Becky to take full advantage of the class. "Everything that happens here is all part of my *commitment*," she told Callum's wife. Looking down at the perpetually moving duo, she couldn't help smiling. "Your girls are beautiful, by the way."

Becky laughed. "I'm kind of partial to them myself," she responded. "I just wish they'd slow down a little bit. They're into *everything*—usually at the same time and in opposite directions. For a while Sasha was the quiet one, but now there's absolutely no difference between them. If anything, she's seems to be trying to make up for lost time."

"Well, this class might just take a tiny bit of the edge off their energy and hopefully tire them both out enough for you to be able to recharge your batteries," Hailey told her. And then she reconsidered her words. "Or at least to catch your breath."

"Oh, if only," Becky said wistfully with a heartfelt sigh. "But by then, I'll have to be back at work," she confided.

Just then, the entrance to the Mommy and Me class opened. As if on cue, Becky and Hailey both turned toward the door. Each was expecting to see Callum come walking into the room.

The next second, Hailey felt her pulse leap a little. Instead of Callum, she saw Dillon coming in.

Hailey immediately regretted that she hadn't worn her more attractive athletic attire. Thinking only of mobility and comfort, she'd put on an out-

fit that she had to admit had seen better days. The
only consoling thought here was that the light blue
outfit she had on had come to look this way because she had worn it while doing one of her many
workouts. For the spa's first month, she wanted to
look like a hands-on manager who used the facili-
ties herself. She felt that this made her look more
approachable, as if she, her staff and her patrons
were all one big family.

"Dillon," Becky said the moment her brother-in-
law had joined them. "What are you doing here?"

The second he had reached them, Sasha and
Luna began to climb all over him as if he was a
living, breathing jungle gym.

Moving carefully so as not to dislodge his tiny
climbing monkeys, Dillon dropped down beside
the nurse that his brother had had the good fortune of marrying. "I'm here to tell you that Callum
sends his regrets but he's been unavoidably de-
tained at a building site. He sent me to temporarily
take his place until he's able to get here himself."

Becky looked at her brother-in-law a little skep-
tically. "Are you sure that you know what you're
in for?"

Placing a protective hand on the twin who had
managed to climb up onto his forearm, he gently
guided the little girl back to the floor. "Haven't a
clue," he confessed. "Callum said something about

this being a gym class for toddlers. How hard can it be?" he asked, although he was beginning to see that maybe he had underestimated the assignment.

"It's not a gym class," Hailey told him, flashing a smile as she stepped in to greet him. "It's a yoga class for moms and their kids."

"Moms?" Dillon repeated. That wasn't what Callum had told him. "Then why am I here?" he asked, confused.

"It's also for dads," Hailey quickly told him.

Dillon still looked a little skeptical. That didn't sound right to him. "Yoga for dads?"

"Yes. It's really very beneficial," Hailey assured him. She was trying hard not to laugh. Not at his stance, which admittedly was a bit awkward, but at the way his nieces seemed to regard him as a piece of equipment. "Yoga has been found to really help you relax. I don't mean you specifically," she quickly corrected herself. "I mean people in general."

Out of the corner of her eyes, she could see the rather amused expression on Becky's face. She couldn't help wondering if that was in response to Dillon looking like a fish out of water, or if there was another reason for the woman's amusement.

She had to admit that having the little girls climbing all over him did look pretty funny. The fact that he endured it without protest spoke well of him.

"And Callum knew this?" Dillon asked, looking at his sister-in-law. "That this was a yoga class?"

"He did," Becky confirmed, doing her best to try to maintain a straight face.

Dillon sighed, resigned. "Well then, I guess I can give this a shot."

"Good for you," Hailey said, pleased as she tried to cheer him on.

Dillon's expression indicated that he wasn't all that sure about what was about to happen, but he had committed himself to this and he wasn't about to backtrack, at least not in front of witnesses.

Because he'd been somewhat forewarned about the nature of this class, Dillon had stopped in the locker area to change out of his suit and into a pair of shorts, a comfortable pullover and a pair of sneakers. He definitely didn't look at home in any of it.

Apparently he noticed the way Hailey was looking at his foot attire.

"Callum said I needed to wear something other than boots," he explained.

"Ah, so you made the ultimate sacrifice for your nieces," Hailey concluded. Her smile was wide as her eyes sparkled. "Very noble of you."

Coming from someone else, Dillon would have

taken it as sarcasm. But there was something about the way the woman smiled when she talked that softened everything and pulled him in. He couldn't take offense.

Shrugging, he told her, "I didn't want to scuff up your floors."

Hailey inclined her head by way of acknowledgement. "The floors and I thank you." She looked over toward the instructor in the center of the room. "Looks like you're about to get started," she warned Becky and Dillon.

Becky and her brother-in-law each took a twin's hand. The girl that Becky was holding onto looked disappointed to have her connection to her uncle broken.

"I really appreciate this, Dillon," Becky told him.

He shrugged off Becky's thanks. "Don't mention it."

He slurred the statement a little because Luna, having shimmed up his leg, was now trying to stick her fingers into his mouth.

Apparently, Hailey judged, the little girl was plucking at her uncle's face, trying to make her uncle's smile wider.

"Luna, honey, Uncle Dillon doesn't want to smile right now," Becky prompted.

The little girl looked up at him questioningly,

then pushed even harder at Dillon's mouth, determined to make him grin as Becky tried to entangle the twin from her brother-in-law.

Hailey tried her best not to laugh, but it wasn't easy. "I'd say you definitely have your hands full," she said as she began to back away.

"You're going?" Becky asked, sounding just a touch distressed.

"Unless you'd like me to stay," Hailey told her. She had gotten the impression that Dillon would have rather that she wasn't around to witness what he was about to go through.

"Please," Becky said.

The hopeful look on Becky's face overrode what she assumed might be Dillon's wishes in the matter. After all, he hadn't said anything.

"Then I'll stay," Hailey replied.

Glancing in his direction, Hailey couldn't tell if Dillon took her decision in stride, or if her presence put him on edge.

She supposed she would find that out soon enough.

Chapter Six

She had learned something today, Hailey thought, smiling to herself. She had learned that, without a shadow of a doubt, Dillon Fortune was an incredibly patient man.

She had been watching Sasha and Luna's *Unca Dilly* contort his body into all sorts of really awkward, uncomfortable positions for the last half hour, simply to entertain his sister-in-law's two little girls.

Some of the movements he'd attempted, like virtually making a pretzel of himself, could *not* have been easy for him. Hailey was fairly certain that at least half the moves he attempted had to have really hurt.

In her opinion, the movements he was doing would have been challenging for an accomplished yoga instructor to execute.

But Dillon had gamely tried each and every one of them as they came up. Some movements he'd attempted had come with accompanying sound effects. Those too had been for the girls' gleeful benefit. The twins had lapped it all up like hungry little puppies. Entertained, they had giggled to the point that they had fallen down—and then they had giggled some more.

It was clearly obvious to anyone who was watching that Sasha and Luna really loved their uncle.

They weren't the only ones, Hailey thought. She found herself thinking that the contractor was just adorable, willingly doing all this just to keep the twins entertained.

If it hadn't been for the twins, Hailey was fairly sure that she would have never been privy to this kinder, sillier side of the handsome contractor. While she was attracted to the former, she found *this* Dillon Fortune to be utterly endearing.

Her only problem was that she kept staring too much.

But she really couldn't help it. Every time she tried to look away, Dillon did something else to make his nieces laugh and she found she just couldn't take her eyes off him.

When she managed to avert her eyes, she noticed that Becky looked a great deal more relaxed now than she had when she had first walked in.

The man was definitely a miracle worker, Hailey thought, even though she suspected that, if he was human, he just *had* to be counting the minutes until the class was finally over.

And then, inevitably, it was.

The moment Linda Hathaway, the woman who was running the class, declared, "That's it for today, Moms and Dads. See you all on Friday." Dillon, already on the floor because of the last exercise he had attempted to do, completely collapsed and seemed to all but press his exhausted body flat, practically sinking into the exercise mat he was on.

"Oh, thank God," he murmured, barely audible. "If I had to contort myself into one more position, I think I would've wound up breaking up into a hundred pieces," he groaned for the benefit of his pint-sized captive audience.

Sasha and Luna might not have understood all the words, but they did understand that *Unca Dilly* was out of oomph. The little girls gathered around him on either side, giggling, and then they finally lay down next to him, curling up against him.

"I really appreciate you doing all this for Sasha and Luna," Becky told her brother-in-law. She gently tried to prod the twins to get them up. "C'mon, girls, your uncle's exhausted. You need to give Uncle Dillon a little breathing room."

But the girls stubbornly remained where they were, apparently content to be lying next to their beloved, funny uncle forever.

"That's all right, Becky. Don't worry about it. Leave them where they are right now. I can breathe," Dillon told her.

Even so, Dillon did sit up, although he made no attempt to rise to his feet and move away from the little girls.

"You certainly have the patience of Job," Becky marveled, making no effort to hide how very impressed she was with her brother-in-law.

"The girls are very lucky to have someone like you around," Hailey remarked, adding her praise to Becky's. "You're really a natural born father," she told him with enthusiasm.

Dillon looked at her sharply. Rather than take her words as a compliment, the way she had intended, she saw Dillon's face darken in response. Not only that, but he seemed to withdraw and totally shut down right before her eyes.

Hailey's comment had hit far too close to home,

Dillon thought. And just like that, it had brought with it all sorts of thoughts, not to mention regrets, that he was trying his best to at least bury temporarily, at least until he was able to do something about the situation.

But right now, given this resurrected frame of mind, he needed to leave. Otherwise, he was afraid he'd wind up bringing the little girls down and that was the last thing he wanted to do.

Hailey saw the change in Dillon immediately.

Stunned, Hailey could only wonder what had triggered it.

For heaven's sake, she had given the man a compliment, not verbally filleted him, she thought, at a loss.

Confused, when Hailey looked at Dillon's sister-in-law for some sort of an explanation or enlightenment, Becky only shook her head, a blank, bewildered expression on her face.

Obviously Becky didn't understand his reaction any more than she did.

She was on the verge of asking Dillon what she'd said that was so wrong, but now that the class over, he gave her the impression that he was going to leave.

Immediately.

His next words, addressed to Becky, confirmed her impression.

"I've got to get going, Becky," he told his sister-in-law. "You'll be okay?"

"Yes, of course," she told Dillon with a weary smile.

But his nieces, it seemed, had another opinion on the matter. Each little girl grabbed hold of one of Dillon's arms clinging like limpets to keep him from leaving.

Although he clearly doted on the girls, Dillon looked resolved. He was leaving.

Bending down to the point that he appeared to be folding up his large frame, Dillon kissed the top of each twin's head.

"I'm afraid I have to go, girls. But I'll be back," Dillon promised. Taking hold of one of the girls' hands, he gently tried to extricate himself from his tiny rabid fan club.

As he made progress with one, the other little girl would grab onto him, giggling as if this was a fine new game she and her sister were playing.

"C'mon, girls, let go of your uncle," Becky said a bit more forcefully than the way Dillon had expressed his feelings. "He'll be back soon. Won't you, Uncle Dillon?" she asked, looking at her brother-in-law for his confirmation.

"You bet," Dillon responded. But even so, when

he tried to pull his hands away, his nieces continued to hold onto him for dear life.

Hailey sensed that she had to come to the rescue to keep this from ending with the little girls in tears.

"Hey, how would you girls like some ice cream?" Hailey asked, saying the word *ice cream* as if it were the most wonderful treat imaginable and theirs exclusively to enjoy.

That seemed to do the trick. Letting go of their uncle's hands, the twins eagerly gathered around Hailey, their eyes huge with anticipation.

"Well, you're in luck. I just happen to know where we can find some." Hailey glanced over toward Becky. "Is it okay, Mom?"

Becky laughed. "How could I say no?"

"Well then, come on. Let's go get these hardworking little ladies some well-deserved ice cream," Hailey coaxed for the twins' benefit.

As she herded the girls toward the spa's designated kitchen area, she glanced over her shoulder toward Dillon. She expected to see him watching them.

Hailey was disappointed to see that he had used the opportunity to make good his escape. He was clearly anxious to get away, and although it could all very well be connected to his business, she couldn't shake the feeling that it had something to do with what she'd said.

But how could what she had clearly meant to be a compliment have had such an adverse effect on Dillon?

And why? What did he think she meant by it?

Hailey suppressed a sigh as she led the little girls and their mother into the kitchen. It just made absolutely no sense to her.

But she intended to find out, she promised herself. Her curiosity had been aroused and she wasn't one of those people who was content to just let things go. She wasn't going to be happy or know any peace until she had an answer.

She began by asking Becky.

"Do you have any idea what made your brother-in-law suddenly turn tail and run like that?" Hailey asked as soon as she had handed ice-cream cups to Becky's daughters after first carefully pulling off the tops. She also presented each little girl with a small spoon and armed herself with a lot of napkins for the cleanup she knew would be ahead.

"Well, he didn't exactly run," Becky tactfully pointed out. "And he did say that he had to be getting back, probably for the same reason that Callum couldn't make it here in the first place," Becky surmised.

Hailey thought about letting the matter drop, but her curiosity just wouldn't let her.

That was why, in the next moment, she heard herself asking, "Do you really think that?"

Becky neatly turned the words around without appearing to be argumentative. "You don't?"

"I'm not really sure what to think," Hailey confessed honestly. "One minute, Dillon is all but cavorting with your kids, acting like just another big kid himself. The next minute, he's acting like a dark rain cloud about to let loose with a deluge, all because I paid him a compliment." She rolled what she'd said over in her mind, searching for what might have offended him about the words she'd used.

Coming up empty, she decided to say her comment out loud, hoping that might trigger something for Becky. "I said that he had the makings of a really great father. Why would that upset him? It's obvious that Dillon likes acting the part."

Hailey looked at Becky, waiting, but the latter only shook her head helplessly. "I'm afraid I have no idea. I really don't know very much about Dillon." She smiled ruefully at Hailey. "I'm still learning things about Callum," she confessed.

Hailey felt guilty about prodding the woman. Heaven knew Becky had more than enough to deal with between her job, her new marriage and her little girls.

"I'm sorry, you're right. I have no business playing twenty questions with you about Dillon. He probably misunderstood what I was saying to him." She waved away the whole thing as if she could literally erase it with her hand. "Forget I said anything," she told the new Mrs. Fortune.

Getting up from the small snack table, Hailey handed Becky the fistful of napkins she'd grabbed earlier. "For cleanup," she explained, nodding at the twins. "Although it does look like they managed to get a little bit of ice cream into their mouths," she deadpanned.

Becky laughed, wiping the mouth of the twin who was closest to her.

"That's better than they usually manage to do," she told Hailey. "I'm just glad you gave them vanilla instead of chocolate. It always looks so much messier with chocolate ice cream. I can't wait until they grow out of this phase and they can eat like normal people without creating such an awful mess."

Hailey nodded as she took possession of the used napkins that Becky was discarding. "I understand, but I also know that according to some more seasoned mothers I've talked to, you are going to look back someday and miss this."

Becky sighed as she rose, taking each semi-cleaned twin by the hand. "I know that you're probably right. But I sure would like the chance to find that out for myself," she said, then tagged on the word, "Soon."

"The next Mommy and Me class is the same time on Friday," Hailey said, calling after the departing woman.

Looking over her shoulder, Becky promised, "I'll be here."

Hailey couldn't help wondering if that meant that Dillon would be coming with Becky, as well. Or had her comment about fatherhood scared him away from here permanently?

Get over yourself, Hailey. If the man doesn't show up, it's because his brother was able to take his place. Or rather, take his own rightful place. Callum's the one who married Becky, the one who adopted the twins. Not Dillon.

Hailey sighed as she walked away, heading to another part of the spa. There was no doubt about it. She could all but hear Janelle's voice in her head, telling her that she was spending much too much time thinking about Dillon. It was energy that was better spent elsewhere.

But that being true or not, Hailey couldn't help thinking and wondering about the elusive Fortune brother. She still didn't know very much about him other than the general information that was available about all the Fortune brothers who were currently working hard renovating and building up the town of Rambling Rose.

She knew that Dillon hailed from Florida, a good place, in her opinion, to be *from*, if for no other reason than the place was rumored to have mosquitoes you could put a saddle on and ride.

She also knew that he was part of a far larger family than the seven siblings he had mentioned, although it seemed to her that having seven siblings was definitely large enough for anyone. He was involved in the construction company with his brothers, but unlike Steven and Callum, she didn't have a clue what the man's marital status was,

Was his family covering for Dillon for some reason?

No, that didn't seem possible. Ellie didn't strike her as being a devious person.

Neither, for that matter, did Becky. If her gut impression meant anything, neither were Steven and Callum. They seemed to be rather genuine if she had to make an assessment of the men.

So what was Dillon's big secret—if there *was* a secret?

And if there was no secret, why had Ellie intimated that he might not be in the market for a woman at this time? Was he recovering from a bad relationship?

More importantly, why had he suddenly grown so quiet and all but run away when she had said that harmless comment about him having the makings of being a good father?

She chewed on her lower lip, feeling confused and bewildered.

None of it made any sense to her.

But that didn't mean that she was going to just let it lay there, waiting for someone to say something in passing that would wind up clearing it up for her some time down the line.

No, Hailey told herself, she fully accepted the challenge of unscrambling this mystery, of getting to the bottom of it and making sense of the situation.

Now.

For some reason, what she had said to Dillon about his making a good father had definitely not sat well with the man. That either meant that he secretly wanted to be a father or he already was one and had made what he probably considered to be a horrible, irreversible mess of the situation.

There was a third, sadder alternative to that. He already had become a father but no longer was one because the child had either died or been whisked away by his or her mother, not to be found again.

But if that were the case, wouldn't one of his brothers have known about that? And if one knew, wouldn't he have shared that piece of information with his wife?

The logical answer to that was yes, but Hailey had a feeling that there was absolutely nothing logical about this case.

Which meant that she wasn't going to have any peace until she was able to find out what the big mystery surrounding Dillon was.

And she fully intended to.

Chapter Seven

Despite her best efforts to focus on all the hundred and one details she had to see to in order to keep the spa in top running condition, Hailey still found herself looking forward to Friday and, specifically, the Mommy and Me class.

And Dillon.

Though part of her knew she wasn't being very realistic, she was hoping that Dillon would once again be at the class, filling in for Callum the way he had initially.

But when Friday rolled around, not only wasn't Dillon there but neither was Becky. In their place, looking very much like a fish out of water, was

Callum. Dillon's older brother arrived a few minutes before the class was scheduled to begin, flanked on either side by one of the twins and doing his best to look as if he was actually up to this challenge.

This was a man who had helmed the purchase of large plots of commercial properties within and around Rambling Rose. Blessed with astute business acumen, Callum had gotten in on the ground floor of what he and some members of his family referred to as the town's "gold rush." He was a contractor accustomed to juggling several projects at the same time, but even with all that going for him, he still appeared to be no match for Luna and Sasha, the two little girls he had adopted when he had married Becky.

One look at the man and Hailey could see that he clearly needed help.

With effort, Hailey put her disappointment at Dillon's absence aside and made her way over to his harried looking older brother.

"You look like you're a little overwhelmed here," she observed with a smile. "Would you like a hand with your energetic twosome?"

He flashed a sheepish smile at the spa's manager and said, "I'd be very grateful for any help you can possibly offer."

Hailey's smile widened. "My pleasure." She turned her attention to the twins. Today they were dressed in matching turquoise leotards. "Hi, girls, welcome back." She tousled one of the girl's hair. "Remember me?"

Two identical heads enthusiastically bobbed up and down.

"Is it okay if I help your dad?" she asked solemnly, addressing each of the twins. "He might not know what to do since he wasn't here last time." Again both little girls nodded. They obviously didn't absorb all the words, but they looked very pleased to be consulted. "Thank you," Hailey said, "I appreciate that." And then, sitting down next to Sasha— she silently congratulated herself at getting better at telling the girls apart—Hailey asked their father, "Where's Becky today? Why didn't she come with you?"

Considering the nurse's busy schedule, Hailey thought that the Mommy and Me class would have been something Becky would have looked forward to as a break in her hectic routine.

"Linus's father, Eric, turned up with Linus at the pediatric clinic this morning," Callum told her, making a grab for Luna who was about to escape and fraternize with a little boy in the row behind them.

Hailey was surprised to hear about Linus's return. Barely four months old, Linus was regarded as quite the celebrity in Rambling Rose since, his mother, Laurel, had gone into premature labor at the opening of the pediatric clinic. Becky and Dr. Green had tended to her before transferring her to the hospital in San Antonio to give birth. From all indications, that would have been the end of the story if Laurel hadn't suddenly reappeared weeks later, only to leave Linus on the doorstep of the clinic.

Stephanie Fortune—Dillon, Callum and Steven's sister—had stepped up to temporarily become the abandoned baby's foster mother. Stephanie had grown very fond of the infant when Laurel's old boyfriend, Eric Johnson, had abruptly turned up to claim the boy as his son.

That had been a couple of months ago and Stephanie, according to what Becky had told her, still missed the infant terribly.

"I thought Eric left town with the baby," Hailey said, looking at Callum.

"He did, but he came back to talk to Dr. Green. Eric's worried about Linus because he doesn't think the baby's growing at the proper rate he should. Becky said that Eric thought it might be because the baby had been born several weeks prematurely, but the baby's father wanted to be sure that there was nothing else wrong so he brought Linus back to be checked out."

Hailey could certainly understand that. "Better safe than sorry," she agreed. Since Callum hadn't mentioned it, she thought she'd ask. "I take it that there's been no word about Laurel's current whereabouts?"

"Nobody's seen Laurel since the day she left Linus at the pediatric center."

When that had happened, it had seemed to Hailey as well as several others that events had come full circle. Or, better yet, that poetic justice was involved. Leaving Linus on the doorstep of the new pediatric center seemed like echoes of the past because the center had been built on the foundation of what had once been the Fortune's Foundling Hospital.

Callum was about to say something else to Hailey, but whatever he intended to say, she never got a chance to hear it. Luna, anxious for his undivided attention, had suddenly pulled on his arm. Caught off guard, because he had been leaning on that arm, Callum almost fell over.

Hailey managed to suppress her urge to laugh at what looked like a comical scene. Instead, she said seriously, "You have to be careful. These little girls of yours are really fast," she warned him. "And they do outnumber you."

"Tell me about it," he said, shaking his head. "I don't know how Becky does it, working all day and then coming home to these two live wires." With one arm around each twin, he hugged both of the girls. "I get worn out just thinking about it."

Hailey laughed. "From what I've heard, moms come with permanently rechargeable batteries," she told Callum. "And don't feel like you need to keep up with Linda, either," she said, indicating the instructor who had just walked into the room. "She's been doing this sort of thing for a few years now. Just do what you can," she advised. "The key thing to remember is to have a good time bonding with your girls."

Callum smiled at Hailey as he nodded. "Good advice," he said just as the class officially began.

She was full of good advice, Hailey thought, settling in to help Callum with his daughters. Too bad she couldn't seem to take her own to heart and stop thinking about Dillon.

But she found that it was hard to stop thinking about the man when their paths kept crossing. Or almost kept crossing. By the time the weekend rolled around, she had just barely missed running into Dillon a number of times.

Just two ships passing one another in the night, Hailey thought philosophically.

She felt frustrated. There had to be some way they could travel in the same direction, at least for a little while, she thought.

"I could sure use a little help here, Janelle," Hailey murmured under her breath the following Saturday morning as she drove to Mariana's weekly flea market. "I'm trying my best to grab onto life with both hands just the way you always told me to," she told the memory of her best friend, "but so far, life seems to just be slipping through my fingers. At least when it comes to Dillon."

She sighed as she continued making her way to the flea market.

Maybe she was being too impatient. Janelle had always said if something was meant to be, it would happen, usually when you were just about ready to completely give up.

"Sure hope you're right about that," Hailey silently said to her friend, "because I'm pretty close to giving up on that hunky cowboy-hyphen-construction guru."

Yes, she wanted to find out what his secret was

and why he had suddenly withdrawn when she had told him he had the makings of being a great dad. But there was a fine line between determination and stalking, and there was absolutely no way that she wanted to accidentally blunder into *that* category.

Okay, she told herself as she reached her destination, she had very little free time to herself these days and there didn't seem to be a letup coming anywhere in the near future. Which of course was a good thing as far as the spa went. But this was an island of time she had managed to cut out for herself and she needed it. She was going to use that time to see what treasures she could find at Mariana's.

Specifically, the treasures she was on the lookout for were frog figurines, something she had started collecting way back in her early teens. Every few weeks, she would hit the flea market, Rambling Rose's very own treasure trove, to see if there were any new figurines there waiting to be added to her personal collection.

Searching through the hastily assembled tables that seemed to go on for endless row after row was both her hobby and her diversion. Just looking through all these things was its own reward, and whenever she actually found a figurine, it was a little like Christmas morning when she was a kid all over again.

She parked her car in the lot that stretched out along the fairground's perimeter. Getting out and eager to get started, she was completely focused on the hunt before her. For the first time in a while, she wasn't even thinking about Dillon.

Which was probably why she didn't see the man until she was practically right on top of him.

Actually, she *was* on top of him, having walked right into someone without even realizing it.

Their bodies collided and it was all she could do to keep from falling down. The only reason she regained her balance at all was because the person she had walked into grabbed her hard by her shoulders in an effort to keep her upright.

Hailey began to apologize before she realized whom she had walked into.

"Oh, I'm so sorry, I didn't mean to—Dillon," she exclaimed, practically doing a double take. Hailey tried to back up and found she couldn't.

Belatedly, Dillon realized he was holding onto her. Not only that, but it took him a second to release his hands from her shoulders. Electricity shot through him, as if holding her like that felt right somehow.

He was going to have to watch that.

"I didn't realize you would be here," she cried, feeling genuinely flustered and more than a little tongue-tied, which was highly unusual for her. "Sorry," she apologized again. "I didn't mean to walk into you like that."

Rather than be standoffish, which was what she half expected, since she'd gotten the impression that he was avoiding her, Dillon looked amused.

"Who did you mean to walk into?" he asked Hailey.

"What?" And then she realized that he was teasing her. She laughed, some of her nervousness leaving her. "Nobody. I was just trying to get my bearings. The people who bring their things to Mariana's Market never seem to be in the same place twice. They're always switching around so it's like a brand new treasure hunt each and every time."

Dillon looked at it from the point of view of a businessman. "They do that so they can try to catch your eye with something new, something you didn't even know you were looking for until you see it."

Hailey looked impressed. She wouldn't have thought a flea market would have any allure for him. "You sound as if you're talking from experience."

"I am. Secondhand experience, actually," he readily admitted. "But still valid in this context.

Steven came here just last month and found this really cool scrapbook while he was browsing one of the stands."

"Oh?" He'd caught her attention even as she continued weaving in and out of the rows, looking at what the various sellers had on display. "What made it so cool?" She couldn't help being curious about what Dillon and his brothers might have found appealing at a flea market.

"It was filled with old articles about the town, you know, the way it was back when it was first built," he told her, following Hailey as she turned down another row. "There was even an article about the old Foundling Hospital—except it wasn't old at the time."

"That sounds really interesting. I'd love to see the scrapbook sometime," she told him in all sincerity.

"Okay, I'll ask Steven about it and see if I can get him to lend it to you." The next row was rather crowded so it took him a moment of weaving in and out before he could continue talking. "He seems pretty taken with the scrapbook himself. Looking through it is like looking into a passageway between the past and the present. I could almost see the wheels in his head turning as he was making more plans for future projects."

Dillon realized that he was going on and on, monopolizing the conversation and not giving Hailey a chance to talk. He supposed that was because of his nerves. He found himself being really interested in her despite all his attempts not to be. "So, what brought you here?" he asked.

Hailey was intently searching for one of the sellers she had connected with the last time she was here. So far, she hadn't been able to find the woman. Preoccupied, she answered, "Frogs."

Dillon abruptly stopped walking and looked at Hailey. "Excuse me?"

She turned to look at him over her shoulder. He looked so stunned that she had to laugh. And quickly followed that with an apology. "I'm sorry, I didn't mean to laugh like that. I'm not laughing at you," she added. "I'm laughing with you."

"But I'm not laughing," Dillon deadpanned.

He looked so serious for a second that she became flustered again. She really didn't want to mess up this rare opportunity, especially since he seemed to be in a good mood and they were hitting it off.

"I'm sorry, Dillon. I didn't mean to imply—"

"It's okay, Hailey, I'm just messing with you," he told her, waving away her apology. "But seriously, you're here looking for frogs?" he repeated. He wouldn't have thought she was the kind who would have wanted a pet frog. She struck him as more of a pet puppy person.

"Frog *figurines*," she clarified. "I come here to Mariana's flea market every few weeks, hoping to find another figurine to add to my collection."

She sounded serious, he thought. "How big is your collection?" Dillon asked.

"Not very big," she admitted. She was familiar with the people in the next row and knew there were no figurines to be found at their tables. Pausing, she looked up at Dillon and answered his question. "At last count, I had almost twenty figurines, all different," she specified, since that was important to her. And then she laughed softly. "You'd be surprised how many of these things there are out there once you start looking."

Intrigued, he asked, "Why did you?"

She didn't quite follow him. "Why did I what?"

"Start looking for figurines of frogs?" he said, supplying the rest of his question. "I mean, it's not something that is typically collected—at least, I wouldn't think so," he amended. He didn't want her to think he thought her hobby was odd—just maybe a little unusual.

Hailey shrugged. "I guess it goes back to when I was a little girl. I always loved the story about *The Frog Prince*. I must have made my mother read that story to me at least a hundred times before I finally learned to read it for myself."

"The Frog Prince," Dillon repeated, still trying to understand the reason behind her fascination. "As in you have to kiss a lot of frogs before you meet your prince?" he asked.

She blushed a little, something that he found instantly endearing. "Something like that," she admitted.

"And did you?" Dillon wanted to know. "Did you meet your prince?"

"No," she admitted, thinking of some of the wrong choices she had made in her life. "Not yet."

"Well, I guess I know how that is," he said, commiserating with her. "Kissing your share of frogs, I mean." When she looked at him curiously, Dillon quickly explained, "I've probably kissed my share of… What's the female equivalent of frogs? Froggettes?" he asked, testing the word out.

For some reason, the word he had come up with really struck her as funny. Hailey started to laugh, really laugh. Hard.

Listening to her, Dillon found himself captivated by the sound of her laughter. So much so that he could feel himself wanting her.

Really wanting her.

Chapter Eight

"You know," Dillon heard himself saying quietly so that no one could overhear them, "I wouldn't mind being one of your frogs." The moment the words had come out of his mouth, he was afraid that they could be misconstrued, or, at the very least, they didn't come out quite right. He didn't want Hailey to think he had lost his mind. Or that he was putting moves on her. That would be too crass. "I mean…"

At a loss, he wasn't sure just how to finish his sentence.

He was shy, Hailey realized, delighted by the very idea. Who would have ever thought that someone as incredibly sexy and good-looking, not to mention talented, as Dillon Fortune could actually be shy?

She smiled at him, doing her best to encourage Dillon to continue his thought—and to act on it.

"I think I know what you mean," she told him.

Was it his imagination, or did Hailey seem to move closer to him without actually taking a single step? Or maybe he had somehow just willed the distance between them to disappear?

Whatever the reason and however it happened, one moment he was looking down into her upturned face, the next moment Dillon was kissing her.

He wasn't the kind of man who believed in engaging in public displays of affection. On the contrary, Dillon had trained himself to behave like an extremely private person, keeping his thoughts as well as his feelings tightly under wraps.

But this was different. He didn't know why it was, he only knew that it was.

So very different.

He had caught himself thinking about kissing Hailey since that first day when she had uncorked that unfortunate bottle of jasmine and wound up christening his shirt with it. That act alone, even though it was unintentional, should have made him extremely wary of her—but it hadn't.

To be honest, nothing she had done had driven him away, even though, under normal circumstances, it would have.

Kissing her now was a totally intoxicating experience.

Damn but she tasted heavenly. Her lips were sweet, like strawberries that had been picked just at the right moment. Not too sweet, not too tart, just incredibly arousing.

Desire shot through Dillon's veins as he deepened the kiss.

Hailey felt herself getting lost in his kiss.

Lord, but he was making her head spin. This was even better than she could have possibly imagined. Her blood was rushing through her body, making her aware of just the moment, just the man and nothing more.

Ordinarily, Hailey was always aware of her surroundings, always aware of everything and everyone around her, no matter what. But this time, Dillon had no sooner kissed her than everything else around them had just managed to vanish, becoming one with the universe as it slipped away into the mist.

Leaving just the two of them.

All she was aware of was this incredible surge within her, this incredible desire to slip away with him somewhere and explore all these wonderful, delicious feelings that she was experiencing. The feelings that were racing through her body, making her want him. Making her want to *be* with him.

And then, finally, because he sensed that they had to undoubtedly be attracting attention to themselves, Dillon reluctantly drew back his head.

He smiled into Hailey's mesmerizing blue eyes. "I take it that's a yes?" he asked the moment his lips were no longer on hers.

Hailey returned his gaze, feeling a little dazed, unable to form a coherent thought or even follow what he was saying to her.

She blinked, struggling to focus her brain. "A yes?" she repeated uncertainly.

Unable to resist, he ran his fingers through her hair, marveling at how very silky it felt to the touch. "To my kissing you."

And then her mind caught up to the rest of her. Hailey smiled at him, the smile unfurling like the first flower of spring raising up its petals to the rays of the warm sun.

Captivated by the sight, Dillon found he couldn't draw his eyes away from her enticingly sexy mouth.

"I wouldn't have kissed you if I didn't want to," Hailey told him.

"Just to be sure you know, you can always say no. That's your prerogative."

"Good to know," Hailey told him. She remained rooted to the spot, hoping for a repeat performance. "Then I choose *not* to say no."

He felt heartened, although there were distant alarms going off in his head, warning him not to take this any further even as he heard himself say, "Would you mind if I asked to see you again?"

"You mean other than here right now?" she asked, her smile growing deeper.

"Yes, other than that," he told her with an amused laugh.

"I'd mind if you *didn't* ask," Hailey told him honestly. "Yes, you can ask to see me again. Just name the time and the place and then we'll coordinate our very busy schedules," she teased.

Then, before Dillon could answer, she surprised him by slipping her hand into his and lightly tugging on it, getting him to come along with her. She was back to weaving her way through the various rows of tables displaying merchandise.

"Are we still looking for those frog figurines for you?" he asked. He wanted to be clear what she wanted him to search for.

"We are," she confirmed. She knew he was thinking about the kiss and how it might very well have been a signal that her days of kissing frogs were over.

Time would only tell if it was. But her days of collecting figurines were still ongoing.

She smiled at him. "I can't very well put you on my shelf, now can I?"

"Well, for one thing, I don't think I'd fit," he deadpanned.

Hailey's eyes slid over his robust body. She felt herself growing warm. "No, you definitely would not. Besides, you have work to do and so do I. That kind of stationary life is not right for either one of us." Her smile went all the way up to her eyes as she told him, "I'd like to think that's something that we have in common."

When he didn't say anything in response, Hailey wondered if he had even heard her. From the expression on his face, his attention was apparently focused on something else.

"Dillon?" she said, raising her voice, but to no avail. He still wasn't looking at her.

Maybe he was having second thoughts about their getting together, she thought. Maybe she had gone too fast, assumed too much.

Maybe—

"There," Dillon said, pointing to something she couldn't see because there were a cluster of people in the way, blocking her line of vision. He was tall enough to see over them.

"There?" Hailey repeated, still mystified. She had no idea what Dillon could be referring to. She didn't see anything around that might be considered out of the ordinary.

Rather than explain what it was that had caught his eye, Dillon suddenly picked her up in his arms and then put her on his shoulders as easily as he would a child.

It was all she could do not to squeal. Hailey struggled to contain her surprise.

"One row over," he told her, then added more specifically. "Look at the display three tables from the end."

Still confused, Hailey looked in the direction he had pointed out, vaguely aware that the milling crowds of shoppers and browsers around her appeared to be mildly entertained by their balancing act.

"What am I—?"

No sooner had Hailey started to ask him what exactly she was supposed to be looking for when she saw it. Stunned, she could only marvel at how she might have missed seeing it if it weren't for Dillon and his high vantage point.

"Oh!" she cried, utterly mesmerized.

"You see it," Dillon concluded, pleased.

Now that she was looking at it, she couldn't understand how she could have possibly *not* seen it. It was a figurine of a frog, all right. Dressed in a black tie, formal black jacket—referred to as tails, she recalled—the frog also had on a black top hat and he was leaning on a striking black walking cane. It looked so vivid, the little frog seemed as if he were about to start dancing at any moment. And if she listened, she could almost swear she could hear the dapper little frog about to break into a song.

"Oh, yes, I see it," she told Dillon with enthusiasm. When the light hit the figurine just the right way, she was certain that the jacket and top hat sparkled thanks to a sprinkling of sequins.

Belatedly, Hailey suddenly realized that he was still holding her up on his shoulders.

"I've got to be getting heavy for you," she said self-consciously. "You can put me down now."

Kneeling, Dillon carefully guided Hailey down from his shoulders, even though he denied the assumption she had made.

"You're not getting heavy at all," he insisted. "Believe me, I've hauled sacks of concrete that weighed a great deal more than you weigh. I put you up on my shoulders because I figured that was the fastest way to get you to catch a glimpse of that frog," Dillon explained to her. "I wanted you to see it before someone else bought it."

"And I really appreciate that," Hailey told him.

As if to prove it, the second her feet made contact with the ground, Hailey immediately rushed between shoppers, making her way over to the next row so she could purchase the figurine.

Dillon made no attempt to stop her or to tell her to slow down. Instead, he just followed in Hailey's wake.

She could move really fast. But then, why shouldn't she? he asked himself. Hailey obviously kept that body of hers in excellent shape with those exercise classes she had put together. He had a feeling that she didn't just stand back and let the instructors do the heavy lifting. She was the type to be there every step of the way, he thought.

By the time he had caught up to her and was at her side, Hailey had concluded negotiating with the older woman who was selling the figurine. The dapper figurine was nestled in with a number of other "treasures" that the woman had brought to the flea market in an attempt to sell.

"Can I interest you in this ancient cameo?" the woman asked, holding the necklace up and waving it slightly before her face.

"No, thank you. All I want is the figurine," Hailey assured her.

"Are you sure?" the woman asked, unconvinced. "After all, a girl can always use another piece of jewelry," the woman told her. She held up the necklace again, as if the second time was the charm.

"Yes, I'm sure. I'm only interested in the frog figurine," Hailey told her. "Now, if you have any others…"

"No, Froggie here is one of a kind," the woman informed her. Her face lit up and as she smiled, it made some of her more prominent wrinkles look as if they were receding and fading away. She gave Dillon a long appreciative look, her brown eyes sliding up and down his body. "Kind of like your fella, here," she told Hailey.

Not wanting Dillon to feel embarrassed or uncomfortable, Hailey quickly denied the woman's assumption.

"Oh, he's not my *fella*. We just ran into one another here this morning."

The older woman's eyes lit up as they gave Dillon a second, even longer appreciative survey. "Then could he be mine?" she asked with genuine interest.

The woman was probably about twenty years

older than they were, possibly more, and behind the smile there was definitely something about her that reminded Hailey of a determined predator. She could almost envision the seller's appetite causing her to all but devour Dillon in a couple of well-placed bites.

Just in case she was right, Hailey decided an ounce of prevention might be called for.

"On second thought, I spoke too soon," Hailey told the woman as she shelled out the money for the figurine. Sparing Dillon a quick wink, she added, "He is my *fella*."

Rather than be annoyed, the woman smiled knowingly as she nodded her head.

"Yes, I thought you might change your mind once you had a chance to think about it," the seller said knowingly.

That had Hailey wondering if she had just been played.

Well, it didn't matter. She had gotten what she wanted: a one-of-a-kind frog figurine in good condition.

After taking her money, the seller carefully deposited the stylish frog into a paper bag. The bag was too small to properly house the frog, but it did manage to cover his legs all the way up to his waist. It also covered up his cane.

"You're good luck for me," Hailey declared with a bright, pleased smile as she looked at Dillon.

"Glad I could help."

He gave the area a quick, final cursory look. "Are we done here?" he asked hopefully, then tagged on "Or—?"

"Or," she told him without any hesitation. "I want to look around a little more and see if I can locate any more frog figurines. And besides," she glanced back at him and his hands, "you're still empty-handed," she pointed out.

"Oh, I wouldn't exactly say that," Dillon responded, his eyes drifting over in her direction.

"Well, I know what I'm looking for," she said by way of conversation. "What are *you* looking for?"

"I think it's a case of I'll know it when I see it," Dillon told her.

Hailey smiled at him with a knowing smile. "In other words, you haven't the slightest idea what you're looking for."

Dillon laughed lightly as he moved his shoulders up and down in an evasive shrug. The shrug told her beyond a shadow of a doubt that she had certainly guessed correctly.

"All right, then," Hailey told him gamely, threading her free hand through his. She glanced at her watch. "I've got another forty-five minutes before I have to get back to the spa. Let's see if we can make the most of that time."

"What happens in forty-five minutes?" Dillon wanted to know, allowing himself to be led around by his shapely tour guide.

"I turn into a pumpkin," Hailey answered him with a wink.

"*That* I'd like to see," Dillon told her, a smile curving his mouth as it seemed to snake its way up to his eyes, as well.

"Stick around long enough and you just might get to witness it," she answered.

"Promises, promises," Dillon responded with a quick wink.

Hailey felt the wink burrow its way directly into her stomach, creating its own little tidal wave as it came to rest there. No doubt about it, the man had a way of stealing her breath away.

Chapter Nine

It seemed nothing short of a minor miracle to Hailey just how she managed to move around the spa for the rest of the day, seeing as how her feet didn't actually make any contact with the floor beneath them.

She really was floating on air.

She had a date with Dillon.

Each and every time she thought of that, her stomach would do a little dance, completely throwing off her equilibrium, not to mention that her stomach wound up tying itself all up in knots. Granted the date wasn't until the end of the week—Friday—but it was a date. An official date that had absolutely nothing to do with her work or his.

At the time, just before they went their separate ways from the flea market, it had taken her a few minutes to realize he was asking her out. Dillon had adorably stumbled through the invitation and at first she hadn't been sure if he was asking her if she liked eating at the restaurant in town, the one he and his brothers were currently involved in renovating, or if he was asking her to eat at Osteria Oliva, the Italian restaurant that had recently opened at the far end of the shopping center. Maybe he wanted a layperson's point of view on the work that had been done.

When Hailey finally unscrambled his words—no easy feat—Dillon had looked almost as surprised as she was at the invitation. It was almost as if the invitation had come out of his mouth of its own accord. But what counted was that it *had* come.

Hailey smiled to herself. The man was definitely *not* a smooth talker, but she liked that about him. The last few men in her life had all been silver-tongued bad boys who, she had found out later in each relationship, had a penchant for juggling more than one woman at a time in their lives.

It had gotten to the point that she had started to think—unhappily—that she had a type, and not a good one. Or, at the very least, that she was prey for a certain type of male.

Her smile deepened as she relived the moment

he had asked her out. When Dillon had finally gotten out the invitation, he would have made the "aw, shucks, ma'am" Gary Cooper type very, very proud.

Hailey found his shyness extremely sweet. It was refreshing. At least she knew when he said something he meant it and wasn't just spouting empty words in an attempt to win her over and talk his way into her bed.

That in itself was more tempting than she would have thought possible. Dillon's utter awkwardness was exceedingly seductive.

But she was getting ahead of herself. She needed to pace herself, to go slow instead of just diving headlong into the waters. Despite all her warnings, though, Hailey could feel her pulse racing each and every time she thought of spending time with Dillon.

Hailey sighed. It was going to be a long, *long* week, she thought.

She was right. It *was* a long week and time just seemed to dribble by one excruciatingly elongated moment at a time.

But finally, *finally* after what seemed like an eternity, it was Friday.

Hailey made plans to leave the spa early in order to give herself plenty of time to get ready for her date. But life, as it was wont to do, had other plans for her, starting with two of her yoga instructors waylaying her just as she was about to leave the building.

It seemed that the instructors were teaching classes with conflicting time slots.

So, with her mind already at home, going through her closet for the perfect outfit to wear tonight, Hailey had to get her thoughts in gear so that she could reschedule the two classes. Once that had been taken care of, she found herself on the phone, calling each one of the prospective clients who had eagerly signed up for the classes.

Hailey was well aware that it was a task that could have easily been delegated to someone else to handle, but since the wellness spa was still in its infancy stage, she felt that it better if she personally expressed her regret to each client. She assured each and every one of them that something like this wouldn't happen again.

In addition, to make sure that everyone involved had their ruffled feathers smoothed, she had given the women who had signed up a discount. It had been an arbitrary last-minute decision on her part and it seemed to have done the trick.

The moment she had finished the calls, she left her office and dashed to her car. Gunning her engine, she glanced at her watch. She was going to be cutting it close, Hailey thought. The relaxing bubble bath she had promised herself had to—out of necessity—turn into a very quick shower.

She still hadn't settled on what to wear, but that too was going to have to be a quick decision rather than one painstakingly arrived at after trying on a variety of different outfits.

She did her best to calm her ever-growing nerves, reminding herself that Dillon wasn't taking her outfit to dinner, he was taking the woman *in* the outfit to dinner. Namely *her.* She had a feeling he would only notice the outfit unfavorably if she came wearing a shapeless burlap sack and a used one at that.

No, she amended, Dillon Fortune would only have an unfavorable reaction to something she was wearing if that outfit had been dipped in a bathtub filled with jasmine oil.

With that in mind, Hailey showered using unscented body wash. She also was careful not to use any colognes or lotions after her shower that had any sort of scent to them. She wanted to take absolutely no chances. The last thing she wanted was for those baby blue eyes of his to suddenly become bloodshot or blurry because of something she had unconsciously put on, washed with or accidentally applied to her skin.

The only thing she wanted to do when the night ended was leave Dillon wanting more.

She hurried through dressing, keeping her eyes on the bedside clock. Dillon struck her as the type of man who arrived early for an appointment, not late.

And, as it turned out, she was right.

Hailey had just finished getting ready by the skin of her teeth. She was in the process of slipping on her high heels when she heard her doorbell ring. Hoping she didn't look like something the cat had dragged in, she hurried to the front door and opened it.

Dillon was standing on her doorstep, looking breathtakingly handsome in jeans, a crisp shirt as blue as his eyes and a pair of tooled riding boots that looked more than broken in.

"You're early," she remarked, trying to cover up the fact that she was staring at him. Belatedly, she remembered to take a step back so that Dillon could come in.

His eyes traveled over the length of her, obviously enjoying the journey. "And you're sensational. I mean…" He found himself at a loss for words.

She grinned, relieved Dillon didn't seem to have noticed her breathless reaction to him.

"No need to correct yourself," she quickly told him. "You can stop right there. It's been a really rough week and an even rougher afternoon and your compliment is more than welcomed," she assured him with feeling. And then she smiled. "Thank you."

"I meant it," Dillon told her. "You *do* look nothing short of sensational." When he saw her reaching for it, he took her shawl in his hands and helped her slip it over her shoulders. "I kind of feel bad that I'm only taking you to the local steakhouse," he confessed. "If I was back in Fort Lauderdale, I could take you to a really classy place, but here..."

He shrugged as his voice trailed off, indicating that he felt at a disadvantage at the shortage of upscale restaurants to choose from.

Picking up her purse, Hailey led the way out. She was eager to put Dillon at ease.

"Well, this really isn't about the food, is it? It's about two people going out so that they can get to know each other better." She smiled at him as she locked her front door. "Right now, all I know about you is that you're part of a construction firm that is busy building and renovating Rambling Rose and that you have very strong shoulders," she added with a laugh.

"Not that strong," Dillon corrected. "You're not exactly heavy."

"Still, that was a very impressive move at the flea market," she told him as they walked to his car. "Speaking of which, I love my frog," she said with genuine enthusiasm. "He's officially the best piece in my collection and if it hadn't been for you, I might have missed him entirely."

Dillon nodded, really pleased by her reaction. "Glad I could help," he responded.

The drive to the restaurant was a short one. Too short to get embroiled in any sort of meaningful conversation.

Dillon seemed to be fine with that. As a matter of fact, Hailey got the distinct impression that he preferred it that way.

But then, she told herself, she was probably reading too much into the stretch of silence that occurred between them.

When they were seated and the server handed them their menus, Hailey noted with a shade of minor distress that all the meals appeared to be centered around either beef or chicken.

Noticing her frown as she skimmed the menu, Dillon asked, "Anything wrong?"

She raised her eyes to his. "Hmm? No, every-thing's fine," she assured him, wanting their first outing to remain positive. "Would you know if this place offers any vegetable platters?"

He looked at her as if her question didn't make any sense to him. "A vegetable platter?" he repeated, a little mystified. "This is Texas. Everything's about meat here, isn't it?"

"Not necessarily," she told him. When she saw that he looked somewhat dismayed by her reaction, she did her best to quickly try to cover it up. "That's all right. I just asked because I was in the mood for something light." She didn't dare tell him she was a vegetarian.

He thought for a second. "Why don't you try the grilled chicken? I hear that's light enough to float right off your plate."

"Well, now you've piqued my curiosity. Okay, I'll give the grilled chicken a try," she said, closing her menu and putting it down beside her silverware.

Pleased that he had solved her problem, he looked back at the menu to double check something, then put it down, as well.

"Well, I know what I'm having." He saw her raise an eyebrow, waiting for him to tell her. "The porterhouse steak. Rare," he added. "With a serving of mashed potatoes and gravy."

"No vegetables?" she couldn't help asking him.

Dillon shook his head. "They'll only take room away from the steak."

It was on the tip of her tongue to say that the vegetables were healthier and if he had his heart set on the steak, he could at least offset his choice with a side of vegetables, but she refrained. The last thing a man on his first date with a woman wanted to hear was a lecture about his food choices.

Instead, Hailey just allowed herself to make a comment about the way he liked his food prepared. "Rare, huh?"

Dillon nodded, blissfully oblivious to her subtle meaning. "Rare," he repeated, then added, "I like my steak barely passed over the flames."

She thought of all the lectures she had attended regarding the health factors of cooking red meat, and wondered whether she ought to suggest to Dillon that he reconsider and have his steak cooked a little more. Well, at least a little more! But she didn't want to come across as lecturing him, and besides, that could be a conversation for another time, in the future.

If they wound up having a future, she silently added.

"So, tell me, what made you want to become a contractor?" she asked once the server had taken their orders and retreated.

Dillon didn't really have to think before giving her an answer. "I guess I like taking old places and bringing them back to life," he told her. "Besides, it was something my brothers were into whole-heartedly." He smiled, remembering. "They have a tendency to jump in with both feet and I'm the one who stops to look at all the possible angles, all the ways something could go wrong. I suppose," he went on as he buttered one of the rolls that the server had left, "you could say that I'm their anchor and my brothers are the ones who buoy me up. In other words," he concluded just before he took a bite of his roll, "we make a good team."

"In *any* words you make a good team," Hailey countered. "But that kind of work has to be rather stressful for you," she said after thinking it over. "If it ever gets to be too much, you might want to look into taking some yoga classes."

His experience at the spa was limited to the Mommy and Me class—and that was really enough in his opinion. Dillon had to laugh. "I think bending into a pretzel would turn out to be more stressful than beneficial for me," he told Hailey. Dillon thought that his response would bring an end to the discussion.

"There's more to yoga than that," she tactfully pointed out.

He shrugged off the point she was attempting

to impress on him. "I'll just take your word for it," he told her.

She eagerly jumped at the opening he'd inadvertently created. "Well, if you'd like to make an appointment, I could personally show you how taking yoga lessons can help you."

He looked at her with surprise. "You think I need help?"

Seeing her error, she quickly restructured her statement. "I think in this fast-paced world, if we're out in it, we all need help."

"Okay," he agreed, gracefully bowing out of what could wind up being a rather lengthy, uncomfortable discussion. "I'll think about it and let you know."

"Can't ask for more than that," Hailey said cheerfully. She could, she added silently, but that wouldn't get her anywhere and the idea was for them to get to know one another, not to antagonize one another. She had a feeling that if she pushed too much, she just might drive Dillon away instead of get closer to him.

She had noticed that when they'd sat down, Dillon had placed his phone on the table right next to his plate instead of tucking it away. Not only that, but she saw that his eyes kept straying to it. He must have done that several times so far and they hadn't even been served yet.

"Expecting a call?" she couldn't help asking.

He hadn't realized that he was being so obvious. "No," he denied. "I just want to be ready in case a call does come in. In this business, you never know," he told her evasively. "Nothing more frustrating than fumbling around, trying to locate a ringing cell phone," he added in an attempt to sweep the subject under a rug. "But if it makes you feel better, I can put my cell phone into my pocket so it doesn't interfere with our dinner," he told her, going through the motions of picking the phone up, even though he was hoping she would say no to his offer. "How's that?"

"Very understanding of you, but if you'd rather keep closer tabs on your phone, please, feel free to do so." She smiled at him warmly. "I take it you can multitask?"

"With the best of them," Dillon told her with a laugh, checking the screen again in case he had accidentally turned down his phone so he couldn't hear it when it was ringing.

But according to the information, there were no missed calls and no text messages, either.

Dillon tried not to show his disappointment.

Chapter Ten

During the course of the meal, as she did her best to draw Dillon out, Hailey discovered that they were more different than they were alike.

Dillon, she found, was a dyed-in-the-wool carnivore who for the most part was a workaholic and he had a tight rein on his emotions. She, on the other hand, was a vegetarian who, while dedicated to her job, was outgoing and liked to live within the moment, getting everything from life it had to offer. She also found out that he liked spending evenings alone while she enjoyed unwinding with friends. She liked reading mysteries while he tended to read architectural books.

No doubt about it, she thought by the end of the evening, they were oil and water. However, she had to admit that they did have one very big thing going for them.

Chemistry. Really hot chemistry.

There was no denying that she was extremely attracted to Dillon and she had the definite impression that he felt the same way.

She felt this even more so when they finally left the restaurant because when Dillon brought her home, he seemed reluctant to leave and have the evening come to an end.

Hailey debated inviting him in for a nightcap and seeing where that led. She really wanted to, but at the same time, she didn't want Dillon getting the wrong impression about her, didn't want him thinking that this was the usual way she did things.

There was nothing "usual" about the way she felt about Dillon. Which was why, despite her promise to herself to the contrary, Hailey was on the verge of inviting him inside when he surprised her by suddenly asking, "Would you like to come and see my ranch next weekend?"

Hailey felt her mouth curving in amusement. "Is that anything like asking me to come and see your etchings?" she asked.

Confused, Dillon looked at her blankly. "What?"

She laughed at his bewildered expression and shook her head. *Definitely from two different worlds*, she thought.

"Never mind," Hailey said, waving away her question. "I didn't realize you bought a ranch."

"Well, technically, I didn't. Not exactly." He searched for the right words. "When we first came out to Rambling Rose to check things out, Callum felt we'd feel as if we all had more at stake and in common with the township if we actually lived here, so we bought The Fame and Fortune Ranch. Jointly," he added. "It belongs to all of us. Callum, Steven, me and Stephanie," Dillon explained when she didn't say anything.

"How do you not get in each other's way living in the same house like that?"

He began to laugh, then realized she might be thinking that he was laughing at her and quickly explained, "I think once you see the place, you won't think that."

"Big?" Hailey asked, assuming that it probably had to be, given that it belonged to the Fortunes.

He was honest with her. "It would have to be downsized for that description to fit." And then he stopped abruptly. "I'm sorry, did that sound like I was bragging?" He didn't want her thinking that he was one of those wealthy men who enjoyed rubbing other people's noses in his wealth.

Hailey laughed again. She couldn't help thinking the man was adorable.

"If anyone else had said that, maybe," she told him honestly. "But coming from you, no. You were just stating a fact for my benefit." Taking a breath, she looked up at him, all sorts of warm feelings rushing through her. "And to answer your initial question, yes, I'd loved to come and see your ranch." She thought about all the work they had done since they had arrived in Rambling Rose. "Did you and your brothers build the ranch, as well?"

"Actually, we didn't," Dillon answered seriously, "although it is brand new. The original owner built it for himself and his fiancée."

"But?" Hailey prodded, then explained, "I sense there's a *but* coming."

"Very intuitive of you," Dillon commented. "They broke up before they ever had a chance to move in together. According to Callum, who handled the transaction, the guy was anxious to get rid of the place and move on, so for the mansion that it is, the cost was relatively inexpensive."

"Mansion?" Hailey repeated, allowing the full import of the word to sink in. If Dillon referred to it as a mansion, the place had to be absolutely *huge*.

Dillon nodded, wondering if he'd said the wrong thing again.

"That's the best way to describe it," he confessed. "There's enough space in the place for each of us to have the privacy we want and not wind up stumbling across the other three if we don't want to." He smiled as he envisioned the ranch. "Not to mention that there are also two guesthouses on the property. And, while the place isn't a working ranch, at least not at the present time, there is a stable on the premises."

"And horses?" she asked, allowing a touch of eagerness to seep through.

He looked down at her, amused. "What's a stable without horses?"

"Empty," Hailey answered automatically.

"Well, rest assured, our stable isn't empty," he told her. "So, now that I've given you a quick history, are you still interested in coming out and seeing it?" he asked, wanting to make sure that he wasn't reading what he wanted to hear into her answer.

"Well, that depends," Hailey told him, doing her best to maintain a straight face.

What sort of a condition could she be putting on this? he wondered. "On what?"

"On whether or not we go horseback riding," she answered simply.

Hailey didn't add that this would flesh out the fantasy she had when she'd first laid her eyes on him and couldn't help thinking of him as the embodiment of a magnificent cowboy.

"Would you like to? Go horseback riding, I mean. Next Saturday," he added. He had planned to build his way up to that slowly once he got her out to the ranch, but since she had brought up the subject now, he figured he'd ask.

"Absolutely," she told him. There was no mistaking her enthusiasm.

"Then it's a date," Dillon told her happily. Eager now, he began making plans in his head. "How early can I come by to pick you up?"

"How early did you have in mind?" she asked. Then, in case he was going to temper his answer because he felt she was the type who liked to sleep in whenever the opportunity arose, Hailey told Dillon, "I'm an early riser."

He broached the hour slowly, not wanting to scare her away. "Is eight too early?"

"Only if I were a slug—and I'm not," she added quickly in case he wasn't certain.

"All right, you pick the time," he told her. He decided it was safer if she got to pick.

"I can be ready by six," she told him, then added, "Earlier if you need me to be."

"No, six is plenty early enough." He rolled the time over in his head. "Tell you what, make it six-thirty in case the horses want to sleep in."

He did have a sense of humor, she thought, relieved as she grinned at him.

"Six-thirty it is," she told Dillon. She decided she needed to wrap this up just in case he wanted to be on his way. "I had a great time tonight," she added.

Dillon smiled at her. "No, you didn't," he said knowingly. "I should have asked you what sort of restaurant you wanted to go to. I guess it never crossed my mind you might be a vegetarian."

Because he apologized, she felt her heart swelling. The men she was used to dating would have blustered through it, saying something about the fact that they thought she was odd rather than apologizing for possibly making her feel uncomfortable. Dillon and she might not have the same tastes, but where it really counted, they were the same. She found that very comforting.

The corners of her mouth curved. He really was very, very sweet. "You're forgiven if I'm forgiven."

Dillon didn't understand what she was saying. "For what?"

"For making you uncomfortable," she explained.

But that didn't really clarify anything for him.

"I'm not uncomfortable," he protested. Then, because he felt as if the woman who had gone out with him tonight could see through him, he added, "Now."

She looked up at him, feeling so very moved that she could hardly stand it.

"Good," she whispered as she stood there, willing him to kiss her.

The next moment, she found that she had the gift of mental telepathy because he did.

Dillon kissed her.

And this time, it was even better than it had been the first time. There were no outside sounds to block, no extraneous noises to filter out. No milling people to ignore.

They could have easily been the only two people in the whole world because, at this moment in time, they really were.

The moment his lips touched hers, her head instantly began to spin, raising her body temperature and accelerating her heart rate.

Sinking into the velvety kiss, Hailey leaned into him, twining her arms around Dillon's neck and wishing with all her heart that she could invite him in.

But for all intents and purposes, this was their first date and she didn't want him to think that this was the way all of her first dates went.

Because they didn't.

Damn, Dillon thought, but she was making things really difficult. Without any apparent effort on her part, she had breached all his barriers, leaped over all of his well-placed walls. One second she was on the other side and then, wham, she was right there, nestling in through a crack he hadn't even been aware existed.

If he weren't careful, he was in danger of allowing her to get in far closer than he wanted her to be.

Even as he reasoned with himself, he had to fight the very real desire to lead her inside and take this date to its natural conclusion.

But just as he felt that he was about to capitulate and lose the battle with himself, Dillon felt his cell phone suddenly begin to vibrate, demanding his exclusive attention.

Without looking at the screen, he knew who was calling.

It had to be her.

Dillon forced himself to return back to earth. Taking a deep breath, he drew his lips away from Hailey's.

"I'd better get going before it's tomorrow," he told her.

But even as he said this, Dillon could feel himself being trapped between a reluctance to leave and the need to go.

Hailey nodded, drawing back.

"Can't have that," she agreed, although she didn't sound all that convinced.

But maybe he was just reading into her reaction, Dillon thought, branding her actions with his own reluctance. He took a deep breath. He needed to stop vacillating and just go before he did something that they were both going to regret for very different reasons.

He began to walk away from her, then turned back and caught her up in his arms for one last deep quick kiss. When she looked at him, stunned because she thought he'd changed his mind about leaving again, Dillon told her, "One more for the road."

And then he was gone.

Forcing herself to move, Hailey slipped inside her house, then closed the door. Once she flipped the lock, she leaned her back against the door and slid down to the floor.

"You are definitely not what I'm used to, Dillon Fortune," she murmured into the darkness.

He definitely *wasn't* what she was used to. But she was really looking forward to finding out what he *was* like.

* * *

The rest of the week spread out before her like an obstacle course to be maneuvered through and conquered with the prize being the man on the other side of that week. Dillon Fortune and his ranch.

She couldn't wait to go riding with him. Couldn't wait to see Dillon looking all masculine and incredibly sexy on top of a horse.

Couldn't wait to see *him*.

Suddenly, every minute was precious to her as it went by because it was one less minute she had to live through before she could finally get to go horseback riding with Dillon.

Telling herself that she was behaving like some smitten teenager didn't make her change her behavior, other than force her to bury it—but only while she was at work.

And even then, some of her clients, the ones who knew her before the wellness spa had ever opened its doors, detected a difference in her behavior, a certain lightness about her manner.

"Someone new in your life?" Maryanne Edwards asked her.

Maryanne had known Hailey since they were both in their senior year in high school. Although not anywhere as close to her as Janelle had been, Maryanne had still witnessed Hailey going through several relationships over the years. She had also seen them all crash and burn for one reason or another.

"Lots of new someones lately, Maryanne," Hailey had answered.

"Let me be more specific," the other woman said, trying again. "Are you juggling two guys at once?" Maryanne asked enviously.

"No, it's more like juggling forty or fifty at the same time," Hailey answered.

When her friend could only stare at her, speechless, Hailey had to laugh.

Taking pity on the woman, Hailey said, "Clients, Maryanne. I'm talking about clients at the spa. I'm juggling forty or fifty clients at a time—and ready to juggle more."

Maryanne frowned, disappointed. "You know what I mean."

"Yes, I do," Hailey replied. "And if you're asking me if I'm juggling a guy, I can assure you that the answer is no, I'm not. Besides," she continued with feeling, "when would I possibly have time for a new guy when I've got so much work to keep me busy? I have to schedule breathing these days."

"I know you, Hailey," the woman told her. "If you like the guy, you would definitely find a way to fit him into your schedule."

"Ah, you give me too much credit, Maryanne," Hailey told the woman as she began to briskly walk away from her friend.

"Do I?" Maryanne called after her.

Hailey didn't answer her. But she smiled as she kept on walking.

One hour closer to her target.

Chapter Eleven

She had told Dillon that she would be ready at 6:30 a.m. Although she was carefree to a fault, Hailey had made it a point never to keep anyone waiting. Which was why the next morning she was ready by 5:30 a.m.

The last thing she wanted to do was take a chance on having Dillon arrive early, then decide to leave because he didn't want to wait around while she was getting dressed. Not that Dillon struck her as being the impatient type, but the truth of it was, Hailey was not all that sure exactly *what* he was.

While she had to admit that Dillon seemed to be acting less like he was carrying around the weight of the world on his shoulders than when she had first met him, she still sensed that there was something reticent about him. Like he was deliberately holding something back.

But as to what, she didn't even have a clue.

Hailey decided that the easiest explanation was probably that he had been burnt in a relationship by some self-centered, unfeeling woman. As a result, Dillon behaved far more guarded about his emotions than the men she'd known in the past.

But, she concluded, all that did was present her with a challenge. A challenge she was more than happy to take on and vanquish.

If that meant getting up slightly before any self-respecting rooster woke up, well so be it. It was a small sacrifice to make.

To keep her mind off how terribly early it actually was and how much she really wanted to go back to bed, after she showered and dressed for the day at Dillon's family ranch, Hailey busied herself preparing breakfast for the two of them.

Not just a simple breakfast, but one that she felt confident any diner on the East Coast would have been more than happy to put on their counter. She was motivated by his apparent attachment to the state where he had originated from: Florida.

To that end, Hailey made scrambled eggs, toast,

bacon and sausage. She also made pancakes and waf-
fles. By the time she finished, there was definitely
enough on the table to feed a small army. She willingly admitted that she had indulged in overkill, but
she had done it to give Dillon his choice of anything
he might have wanted for the first meal of the day.

In order to ensure that it all kept hot, she put everything on a warming tray that she usually kept
tucked away for use during the holidays.

Hailey had just finished arranging the pancake
stacks on two different platters when she heard
the doorbell ring. She automatically glanced at
her watch.

Surprisingly, Dillon was ten minutes late.

Putting the platters where she wanted them, she
hurried over to the front door.

Then, taking a deep breath and bracing herself,
she smiled and threw the door open.

"Hi," she said, greeting him. "You're later than
you said you'd be. I thought that maybe you had
changed your mind."

"I would have called if I'd changed my mind,"
he assured her. "I just thought I'd let you sleep in
a few extra minutes." He laughed softly to himself, acknowledging his mistake. "I guess I should
have known better."

And then he stopped, taking in a deep breath

and inhaling a number of different aromas, all delicious. He looked at Hailey quizzically.

"Am I interrupting something? What is that fantastic smell?" he wanted to know.

Pleased by his reaction, she smiled. "Breakfast. Come," Hailey coaxed, beckoning for him to follow her as she led the way into the kitchen.

"You made breakfast?" he asked, surprised. He hadn't expected her to do that. He had just thought he was coming by to pick her up.

"I had to," she answered, then deadpanned, "The elves have gone on strike."

He wasn't prepared to see all the food that was laid out on the counter. Dillon was clearly caught off guard. For a moment, he didn't know what to say. And then, when he found his tongue, he told her, "You didn't have to do all this."

"Well, once I got started, I kind of did," she told him. "I wasn't sure what you'd like to eat and I thought it safer just to give you a wide choice." She gestured toward the counter. "Take your pick," she invited, pleased by the stunned expression on his face.

The sight of all that food really did catch him by surprise, especially in light of what he said in answer to her invitation.

"I usually just have coffee," he told her.

"Oh." Hailey struggled not to sound as disappointed as she felt. However, Dillon could clearly hear it in her tone.

Thinking of all the effort she had put into this breakfast—effort she had obviously exerted because of him—Dillon quickly backtracked. "But everything looks so good, I can't just walk away from it." He looked at her, giving her a wide smile. "I'll have to taste everything."

She didn't want him forcing himself to eat on her account. "That's all right, you don't have to."

"Oh, but I want to," he insisted.

Dillon felt that although he might not be up on his dating etiquette, he was definitely up on his manners. He was convinced that it would be bad form to have her go to all this trouble and then have him just take a pass on all of it. Besides, even though he wasn't hungry to begin with, he had to admit that this food did smell pretty damn tempting. He would have had to be dead not to have that aroma arouse his appetite.

Dillon's eyes met hers. "Join me?" he asked.

Hailey flashed a smile at him as she picked up two plates. She handed him one and took the other.

"I'd love to," she told him, turning her attention to the extensive array. "I know there's a trend to skip breakfast these days, but I always felt that a healthy breakfast laid the groundwork for a productive day."

Hailey took a little of everything so that, when she was finished, what was on her plate just equaled a normal sized serving of breakfast. Dillon followed suit right behind her.

"Oh." Hailey had barely sat down when she realized that she had forgotten something.

"What is it?" Dillon asked as he saw her getting up again.

"I forgot all about putting out some dry cereal," she explained. "I didn't know if maybe you would prefer that to this." She nodded at the table.

She really did know how to overwhelm a man, Dillon thought. But then, he had a feeling that this wasn't her first time for that. Any man she would have gone out with would have been overwhelmed in her presence.

He put her mind at ease. "Dry cereal never smelled this good." He nodded at her chair. "Please sit and enjoy this with me."

Hailey liked the way he had put that. She did as Dillon suggested, sinking back down in her chair. She really was hungry at this point.

They ate in silence for about a minute, and then he had to ask, "Do you always go this overboard?"

He nodded at all the food that was still left on the warming tray.

"Only when I'm not sure of my audience," Hailey told him truthfully.

"I thought that maybe your plan was to get me so full I couldn't move," he said, breaking off another strip of bacon and eating it.

"No," she laughed, "No plan. I just prepared everything I could think of."

He wasn't in the habit of overeating, but everything tasted so good, it was hard to get himself to stop. "I guarantee you that once I finish even half of this," he said, glancing down at his plate, "my horse is going to go on strike when I try to mount him."

She had a sudden image of that and found herself grinning. "I highly doubt that."

"I don't," Dillon countered, finishing another piece of toast. "Rawhide has a mind of his own, and whatever is on it, he makes sure you know about it."

"Rawhide?" Hailey repeated quizzically.

"My horse," Dillon told her.

He was volunteering details and she eagerly soaked them up.

"What kind of a horse do you have?" Hailey wanted to know. Then, before Dillon could answer, she held up her hand, stopping him. "Wait, let me guess." She thought for a second, picturing Dillon on his horse. "A black stallion, right?"

"I'm afraid that Zorro claimed that one," Dillon deadpanned.

She ate the last of her scrambled eggs. "All right, what *do* you ride?" Hailey asked.

"A dapple gray."

She had to admit she felt a little disappointed by the image that sprang up in her mind. "Named Rawhide?" she questioned.

"That's the name he answers to," Dillon told her. "Why? Something wrong?" he asked. She had a disillusioned expression on her face.

She lifted her shoulders in a shrug. "His name doesn't suit his appearance."

Her answer amused him. He never thought about the horse's name one way or another. "Well, you can tell him that yourself when we go out riding later today," he teased.

"I didn't mean to sound as if I was being critical." She felt she owed him an explanation for her reaction. "It's just when you said his name was Rawhide, I got this image of a jet-black stallion dramatically rearing up on his hind legs."

Finishing his coffee, Dillon set down his cup. "I don't know about the rearing part, but Rawhide runs a fast mile and he has to be one of the smartest horses I've ever come across."

"Well, I'd really love to meet him," Hailey told him, hoping that she hadn't ruined anything by allowing her fantasy to get the better of her.

"You will," he assured her. Damn, but he felt full, he thought. He shouldn't have eaten as much as he had. "Along with Delilah."

"Delilah?" she echoed.

"Your horse," Dillon told her. "At least she is for today. You did want to go riding today, right?" he asked, realizing that maybe he had assumed too much.

"Oh, yes," she told him. The dapple gray might not be living up to the image she had projected for Dillon, but the bottom line was that they were going to go riding together and that was what she really wanted. "What color is my horse?" she asked, then quickly added, "No expectations. I'm just curious."

Dillon smiled. He was getting a real kick out of this woman. "Tell me, does a palomino work for you?"

Her face lit up with anticipation. "Very much so," she answered with feeling.

Dillon took a deep breath as he looked down at what was left on his plate. He had eaten more than he had thought he could. It had all been exceptionally tasty, but there was only so much he could consume without the risk of exploding.

He raised his eyes and looked at her. "Would you be very insulted if I didn't finish everything?"

She laughed softly. "I'd be surprised if you did. I told you, I didn't intend for you to eat everything. I just wanted to give you a variety to choose from."

"Well, you certainly did that," Dillon told her. He rose, picking up his plate and cup and heading for the sink. "You ready to go?"

"Since five-thirty this morning," she told him. Suddenly realizing what he was doing, she said, "You don't have to do that." Hailey began to take his plate from him, intending to put it on top of her own and bring them both to the sink.

But he raised his plate up out of her reach. "My mother made a point of teaching us all to clean up after ourselves. I might be a Fortune, but that doesn't mean I think I'm entitled to special privileges."

Despite their different tastes and approaches to things, she was beginning to really like Dillon and the way he thought.

"Just put your dishes into the sink. I'll wash them when I get home," she told him. Turning her back on him, she unplugged the warming tray and deposited what was left of breakfast into plastic containers and put those into the refrigerator.

When she turned back around to face Dillon, Hailey saw that he hadn't listened to her. He had not only brought the plates over to the sink, but he had washed said plates and was now putting them on the rack to dry off.

"You know, I could get used to this. You're spoiling me," she told him.

In her opinion, the smile that curved the corners of his mouth was positively sexy. "I could say the same thing about you making all that breakfast for us this morning," he said.

She gave him a look. "It's not the same thing. I like to cook," she emphasized. "And if you tell me that you like to wash dishes, I'm going to have to fight a very strong urge to tell you that you're lying."

Dillon grinned, clearly tickled. "Then I won't say it."

Time to change the subject, she decided. "I believe you said something about your ranch and us going horseback riding?" she prompted.

His grin widened as he dried his hands on a nearby dish towel. "I believe I did, yes," he agreed.

She took off the apron she'd had on and draped it on the back of a chair. "Then let's get to it," she urged. "I can't wait to meet Delilah."

"Okay, then let's not keep her—or you—waiting," he said, ushering her toward the door.

* * *

Hailey wasn't prepared for the ranch. She thought she was, but when she actually was able to see it, she realized that the sprawling house exceeded her wildest expectations.

As they came closer, she let out a low whistle. "You people really live in that?" she asked in awe.

"Yes, why?" he asked, amused by her reaction.

This was bigger than huge, she couldn't help thinking. "What happens when you forget to bring your GPS with you?" she wanted to know.

Dillon began to laugh. "It's not *that* big," he told her.

"No?" she questioned. "In comparison to what? New York City?"

Still laughing, he shook his head. "You're exaggerating."

"Not by much," she countered. "Don't get me wrong, I'm sure it's gorgeous on the inside. I'm just used to something a little homier. Something I wouldn't wind up getting lost in," she added.

"Do you do that a lot?"

"Not until now," she answered, looking at the mansion again.

"Then let me take you on a tour of my wing," Dillon offered.

She didn't bother hiding the stunned look on her face. "You have a wing," she marveled.

"Well, it's more like a suite, but yeah. We each do," he told her. "Remember, I told you that when I said we bought the ranch," he reminded her.

She did remember his saying something to that effect. "I guess maybe I didn't really take you literally," she told him.

He didn't understand why she wouldn't. "I don't make things up," he told her.

"I'm beginning to learn that," she said. "Tell me more," she urged.

Because he didn't know when she would want to go back home, he left his car parked in the circular driveway and then got out.

"I will. On the tour," he promised. Rounding the hood, he came up to her door on the passenger side and then opened it without any fanfare. As she began to get out, he offered her his arm.

She had assumed that his formal politeness would fade after he had gotten used to her, but apparently she was wrong. His behavior gave every appearance of continuing indefinitely.

Heaven help her, but she had to admit that she rather liked that.

Chapter Twelve

The outside of the main house that Dillon brought her to was breathtakingly huge, but that still did not prepare Hailey for what she saw on the inside.

Stepping through the massive doorway into the biggest ranch house she had ever seen.

"Wow." The word seemed to escape her lips of its own accord as she looked all around her, taking her surroundings in. It was hard not to be overwhelmed.

As he began to take her on a tour, Dillon tried to see the house he had been living in for the last few months through Hailey's eyes.

He had to admit that he envied her being able to

feel such awe. He tried to remember the last time he had felt anything remotely akin to that.

Maybe when he was a kid?

But probably not even then, he decided. Dillon was fairly certain that what he had felt was nothing like what Hailey was experiencing, judging by the expression on her face.

"I take it your *wow* means that you like it?" he asked, amused.

Hailey drew in a deep breath, and then another when the first breath didn't seem sufficient enough to help her put her thoughts into words.

When she finally spoke, it was to tell him, "I don't think *like* begins to even remotely describe something like this. I mean I've never thought of myself as being sheltered, but this—" she turned around slowly, taking in as much as she could of the expansive area "—this is a completely different world than anything I've ever known." Looking around again, she tried to envision her own home nestled in here. "I think I could fit my whole house—and then some—into what you refer to as a *wing*."

Amused, Dillon laughed. "You're exaggerating," he told her.

"No. I'm not," she insisted. "You grew up in a house like this?" she asked as they continued on their tour, passing a massive bedroom and an equally sized game room followed by a den.

"I grew up in a house," he said vaguely. "With my family." He deliberately stressed what they had in common, not their differences. "And now I am going to take a lovely spa manager—"

"I don't know about the lovely part," she murmured, embarrassed.

"I do," he assured her. "And I'm still taking you horseback riding—unless you'd rather continue the house tour."

"Definitely horseback riding," Hailey declared. "I pick horseback riding."

Dillon laughed, nodding. "Good choice. All right, let's head over to the stables. Are you game to walk over there, or would you rather we drive?" he wanted to know, giving Hailey a choice.

When they approached the property, she hadn't noticed where the stables were. Since everything on the property appeared to be so sprawling, she didn't want to bite off more than she could chew right from the beginning.

"Just how far away are the stables?" she tactfully asked.

He thought for a moment. "About a half a mile," he judged. "Maybe a little more."

She gave him a look that seemed to ask if he thought she was some sort of fragile flower. She could do that distance with one leg tied behind her back, she thought.

"I'll try not to be insulted—and we'll walk," she informed him.

Dillon's smile spread across his lips. "Whatever you say," he told her.

"There's no sense in letting a beautiful day like today go to waste," she said, as if that was what had made her decide on walking there.

He grinned. "Ah, a lady after my own heart," he responded.

Oh, if you only knew.

Like his house, the stable turned out to be massive, as well. So far, it was only half filled with horses. But from what she could see, it looked as if there were no two horses that were alike.

"Are all these yours?" she asked Dillon in awe as she moved around the well-maintained stable.

"Yes," Dillon answered, "the horses belong to all of us in the family. And we keep some on hand for company."

Hailey was impressed. That was happening a lot lately, she realized. "Do you ride a different horse every day?"

"I hardly have time to ride every day. In fact, I don't ride nearly as much as I'd like," he confessed. "This is actually a treat for me. Nothing makes you forget your troubles faster than being on the back of a horse, feeling the wind in your hair, the sun

in your face and, riding with no particular destination in mind, just to enjoy the ride."

He really sounded as if he meant that, she
thought. Apparently there was something that he
really enjoyed doing outside of making the struc-
tures that he drew on paper come to life. She liked
that, she thought. It made him seem more human
somehow.

Her eyes fell on the dapple gray stallion. Her
heart beating hard, she crossed over to his stall.
Because the horse didn't really know her, Hailey
approached the animal slowly. She raised her hand
very carefully toward his muzzle, and then, when
the stallion didn't pull back, she petted him. She
was really pleased that he didn't move his head
back but accepted the contact.

"So who rides all these other horses?" she
wanted to know.

"My brothers and sister. And their friends—or
spouses," Dillon said, correcting himself. He had
to admit that at times it was still hard for him to
get used to the idea that both Callum and Steven
were married now. And Stephanie was engaged
and living with Acton on his ranch. Not only that,
but Stephanie was ten weeks pregnant, as well. It
felt as his life was just galloping passed him.

Dillon focused on his stallion. "I think Rawhide likes you," he noted with genuine pleasure.

"Of course he does," Hailey responded, running her hand along Rawhide's muzzle. "I'm very likeable."

She wasn't bragging. She had always made a genuine effort to try to get along with everyone, and felt that her attitude just naturally radiated toward everyone, animals included.

Dillon was standing directly behind her. From his vantage point, he could breathe in the natural fragrance of her hair. Despite the fact that he had promised himself that this outing was going to be purely platonic, there was no denying that standing this close to Hailey stirred him.

His thoughts went beyond just taking a simple ride on his favorite horse with a pleasant companion. Moved, he was exceedingly tempted to slip his arms around Hailey's waist and hold her against him.

Not the way to go, Dillon. You can't afford to get involved at this point. Maybe later, when things are all ironed out, but not now. You know that.

For one thing, he wasn't free to get involved with someone here when all he had been thinking about ever since he had arrived in Rambling Rose seven months ago was getting back to Fort Lauderdale.

He constantly had to remind himself of that when he was around this woman. He looked down at her as she patted Rawhide's velvety muzzle, imagining those hands on him.

"He's beautiful," she said as she looked up at Dillon.

"Handsome," Dillon corrected her. "I think Rawhide would prefer being called handsome," he said with a wide grin. "He's a male."

"Sorry, boy, didn't mean to insult your manhood," Hailey told the stallion, playing along. For his part, Rawhide seemed to accept the apology. Hailey smiled, continuing to pet the horse. "I think he forgives me," she told Dillon, pleased.

Who wouldn't?

Dillon wasn't aware that he'd said the words out loud until Hailey turned around to look at him in surprise.

"That's a very sweet thing to say," she told him.

"I didn't—I mean…" Dillon flushed, his tongue feeling thick and cumbersome as thoughts went shooting through his head with the speed of a comet.

Feeling his best bet was to change the subject, Dillon cleared his throat and asked, "Would you like to meet your mare?"

"I would *love* to meet her," Hailey told him. Stepping away from the stallion, she looked around. "Which way to her stall?"

"Delilah is right over here," Dillon answered,

leading Hailey over to another stall. This one was located at the far side of the stables.

The second she saw Delilah, Hailey fell in love.

"Oh, she is beautiful," she exclaimed in awe. Holding herself in check, Hailey carefully went through the same process she'd used with Rawhide in order to get close to and pet this new horse. She grinned at Dillon, looking at him over her shoulder. "And since Delilah's a girl, I can say that," she added, pleased.

"Yes, you can," he agreed. He found himself being charmed despite all his best efforts to remain detached and distant. There was no denying that the woman was getting to him. "Let me know whenever you're ready to go riding," he told her, although for his part, he would have been content just to continue watching Hailey pet her mount.

Hailey's eyes sparkled as she turned them toward Dillon.

"Now. I'm ready now," she informed him with enthusiasm.

"All right, then I'll get them saddled up and we can get going," he told her as he went to get the equipment.

Hailey watched as Dillon returned with a saddle, a blanket and a bridle, setting them down in the stall. Then he did the same for Rawhide. The man did keep surprising her, Hailey thought, leav-

ing Delilah's stall and making her way over toward
Dillon's stallion.

"You saddle your own horse?" she asked.

He laughed at the expression on her face. To
him there was nothing unusual about what he was
doing.

"It's part of the total experience. Why?" he
asked. "What were you expecting?"

Hailey shrugged as she petted Dillon's horse. "I
thought you'd have one of your stable hands saddle
up the horses," she confessed.

He didn't bother to hide his amusement. "In
case you hadn't noticed, despite our last name, we
like to get our hands dirty," he said as he slipped
a bridle on the stallion.

Once he did that, he put a blanket on Rawhide's
back, then placed his prized hand-tooled saddle
onto the blanket. Securing the saddle in place, he
checked each cinch in turn, making sure none was
too tight or too loose.

"Okay, Rawhide's ready to go," he announced,
hitching the stallion's reins onto a post in the stall.
"Now let's get Delilah ready."

"You're going to have to walk me through this,"
she told Dillon, following him into the mare's stall.
"I've never saddled a horse before."

Surprised, Dillon turned around to look at
her. "But you have gone riding before, right?" he

asked, realizing that he had taken some things for granted.

"I have, but they always saddled the horse for me at the stable. I don't own my own horse," she interjected, in case he had gotten the wrong impression.

"Well, don't worry. I was planning on saddling your horse for you, too," he told her.

"Thanks, but I'd rather you just showed me how to do it," she said. When he looked at her, she added, "This way I'll know how to do it the next time."

She was planning on a *next time*, he realized. As for him, he wasn't planning on anything beyond this afternoon that they were going to be spending together.

For a second, he thought of saying something to make her understand that there was nothing long term in the making here. But for some reason, he just couldn't get himself to say the words. Part of him felt that it would wind up terminating this ride before it even happened.

So instead, he just said, "Sure. If that's what you really want, I can show you how to saddle Delilah."

With the same equipment ready—a bridle, blanket and saddle—he got started. Gently holding the mare's head so that it remained still, Dillon talked Hailey through all the steps. As he guided her, she slipped the bridle over the mare's muzzle and ears. Putting a blanket on the mare's back was simple enough, but when it came to positioning Delilah's saddle, that turned out to be a little trickier.

When she first slipped the saddle's strap in through the cinch, she wound up not tightening it enough and the saddle slid when Dillon tested it.

"No, it needs to be tighter," he told her. "Don't worry, you're not going to hurt her," he said, second-guessing what Hailey was thinking.

Getting in behind her, Dillon placed his hands over hers and told her, "This is how it's done." With that, he carefully showed her exactly what she needed to do.

Hailey was independent and preferred doing things for herself, but even so, she could really get used to this, she thought, her eyes slipping closed for a second as she absorbed the moment and the feeling of Dillon's hands on hers.

The close contact generated a warm feeling in the pit of her stomach.

Hailey released the breath she realized she had been holding and then drew in another. "I think I have it," she told Dillon, looking at him over her shoulder.

Her mouth was so close to his, for a split second Dillon was really tempted to give in to the desire that even now was growing more and more demanding.

And he probably would have if a ranch hand hadn't picked that exact moment to stick his head into the stall to look in on them.

"Is everything okay here, Mr. Fortune?" Manny Salazar, the caretaker at the ranch, asked, peering into the stall. "Do you need anything?" He smiled politely at the woman with his boss. "Can I get you anything?"

The answer to the man's first question was yes. The answer to his second one was no. Without his knowing it, the ranch hand had managed to rescue him from making another mistake, Dillon thought.

"No, we're good to go, Manny," he assured the man. "Thanks for asking." He looked at Hailey. "Are you ready to get into the saddle?" he asked, holding the mare's reins in his hand.

"That part I know how to do," Hailey answered with a smile. The next second, she swung herself into the saddle and then took the reins from Dillon. "Now all I need is you—to get on your horse," she added, realizing that her pause, coming where it did, had made for a very awkward moment. Even though what she'd said was true. All she did need was Dillon, away from his obligations, away from all the things that distracted him.

That went for the phone that even now he kept

checking, as if he were expecting some sort of earthshaking notification to come across its screen.

Dillon swung himself into his saddle without bothering to even put his foot into the stirrup. As he leaned over to pick up his horse's reins, Hailey couldn't help thinking that he looked nothing short of magnificent astride the stallion like that. The only thing that could have improved the image he cut, Hailey mused, was if his dapple gray had been a midnight black stallion instead of the color it was.

But even so, she couldn't help thinking, Dillon really was nothing short of magnificent.

And, she thought, as they exited the stable, for the next few hours or so, Dillon Fortune was all hers.

"Ready?" he asked one last time, his entire body poised for the ride.

"Ready," Hailey declared, anticipating the ride ahead of them.

"Then let's go!" Dillon said, kicking his heels into Rawhide's flanks.

Horse and rider took off.

Hailey followed suit, doing exactly as Dillon just had. Within seconds, she happily went flying, right alongside of Dillon.

Chapter Thirteen

Hailey found that the next two and a half hours were absolutely exhilarating. The truth of it was she hadn't been on a horse for at least six months—probably longer—and she was a little nervous about being up to it at the outset. But she had always been naturally agile and happily, the whole thing came back to her within a few minutes.

When she glanced toward Dillon, he didn't look as if he thought anything was amiss about her riding. As with the house, he was involved with acting as her tour guide, showing her the acreage of the entire ranch. That included pointing out the two guesthouses as well as the various stretches of empty land in the vicinity that were just *begging* for something to be built on them.

Hailey made no secret of the fact that she was duly impressed by all of it. But what interested her the most was Dillon's role here and just what his plans were for the future.

"Given all this empty space, does that mean that you plan to build your own place here someday?" she wanted to know.

They were looking down on a particularly lush and coincidentally isolated area of the ranch that looked as if it was just perfect for a ranch house, one that wasn't ripe for the label *mansion* but a place where regular people—people like her, she couldn't help thinking—could live.

Dillon appeared surprised by her question. "No, I'm not planning on staying here," Dillon answered matter-of-factly.

Hailey told herself that his response shouldn't have made her feel as if she'd been squarely hit by a Mack truck—but there was no getting away from the fact that it did.

Doing her best to sound nonchalant, Hailey asked, "Oh? You're not?"

"No." He had always thought of his move here as being just temporary because of what he had left behind in Florida. "Once our construction projects here are finalized, I'm going to be moving back to Fort Lauderdale."

The question rose to her lips before she could think to stop herself. "What's in Fort Lauderdale?"

Dillon glanced at her. He'd already said too much, he thought. Consequently, his answer was evasive. "It's my home."

His home. He lived there. That should have been the end of it for her. But Hailey was nothing if not stubborn and she wasn't ready to just let the subject go. "Maybe you'll change your mind."

Dillon didn't want to encourage Hailey, especially since what he had just said was essentially his game plan. He just wanted to finish up here, however long it took, and then move back to Florida. But then, on the other hand, it didn't seem right to flatly rule out the possibility, however minutely slim, that he'd be staying on here in Rambling Rose indefinitely.

Technically, indefinitely was different from permanently, right? he reasoned, slanting another look at the woman beside him.

So he shrugged and said, "Anything is possible."

The smile she flashed him made his wavering definitely feel worth it. Heaven help him, but looking at her made him feel as if the sun had suddenly lit up all his insides.

When he and Hailey finally turned their horses back toward the stable another hour later, Dillon had to admit that he was impressed by Hailey's stamina. She had kept up with him the entire time and she never once made any noises about going back or being too tired to go on. He, on the other hand, had begun to feel himself flagging. He blamed it on the fast pace he'd been keeping up, but whatever the reason, it did bother him a little that he was the one who decided to call an end to their horseback-riding adventure instead of Hailey.

"You might have a little trouble walking when we bring the horses back to the stable," Dillon warned her.

Hailey looked at him, confused. "Trouble walking? What do you mean by trouble?"

"Well, you made it sound like you don't go riding very often and you did just spend almost three hours in the saddle. All I'm saying is it's all right if, when you get off and you find everything aching, you want to complain about it," he told her.

"I don't believe in complaining," she answered truthfully. "Complaining about something is non-productive. Better to put that energy into something useful. Something that could make the situation better."

Dillon looked at her uncertainly. "Are you usually this utilitarian?"

She laughed softly. "No, you caught me on a good day. Most of the time I'm just being annoyingly upbeat—or so I've been accused by grumpy people."

Her answer amused him. "I'd say that compared to you, most people would seem to come across as grumpy," he speculated.

Maybe it was the way the sun was lighting up the area, but Dillon could have sworn her eyes were literally sparkling as she told him, "You'd be surprised. And, just in case you're right about my legs being shaky, why don't you stay close when I dismount? That way, if I am wobbly, you can keep me from falling down flat on my...pride?" she said, substituting the word *pride* at the last minute for the one she really meant.

Dillon nodded, game. "You've got a deal," he told her.

And he kept his word. When they reached the stable, he dismounted first and was right there beside her horse as Hailey prepared to get off Delilah.

Swinging her leg over the mare's flanks, Hailey dismounted the horse in a single fluid motion.

With her feet firmly on the ground, she let go of the breath she was holding.

"See, my legs are perfectly steady," she told Dillon, turning toward him. However, as she began to take a step, she suddenly felt herself all but sink to the ground.

Or she would have if a pair of very strong arms hadn't instantly closed around her and managed to keep her upright.

"Maybe not so perfectly," Dillon judged, his breath ruffling her hair and grazing her cheek as he spoke. "Your legs seem to be a little wobbly," he observed.

Hailey could feel her heart racing again, but definitely in a good way, she thought, grinning up at the man holding her up.

"I guess I stand corrected," she admitted. "My legs don't exactly feel weak so much as they feel… bowlegged," she finally said, describing what she felt to the best of her ability.

"That's because you had them wrapped around the flanks of a horse for a lot longer than you were probably accustomed to." He realized that he could go on holding her like this indefinitely as he smiled down into her face. "Nothing to be ashamed of," he added.

"I'm not ashamed," Hailey protested, then qualified her initial response. "Well, maybe I *am* a little embarrassed."

His smile widened. "Don't worry, your secret's safe with me," he promised.

Then, because he was still holding her far too close than he reasoned was safe for either one of them, Dillon told himself he needed to release her.

And he had every intention of doing just that.

But for some reason, his arms remained exactly where they were. The only thing that did move was his head. He inclined it, causing his lips to be just close enough to Hailey's so that he could do exactly what he had promised himself he wasn't going to do today—or at all in the foreseeable future.

He kissed Hailey.

Dillon told himself that he only meant to brush his lips against hers. But he quickly learned that the best-laid plans often didn't go the way they were meant to. Because once his lips made contact with hers, he really had no choice but to deepen the kiss.

Deepen it to the point that he felt himself getting lost in it.

Getting lost in her.

It took everything Dillon had not to allow himself to sink so far into this kiss that there would be no coming back. No course to take but the inevitable one.

He wasn't that kind of a man, Dillon told himself. He never had been. That meant that he didn't believe in just availing himself of carelessly going the "love 'em and leave 'em" route. He was far too decent a man to take what in his heart he knew could so easily be his. Especially since he intended to ultimately walk away from Hailey. Things being the way they were, he had no choice but to do that.

So, with effort, Dillon forced himself to draw back. To take a breath and tell himself that what he was doing was for the best.

"So," he finally said when he was able to speak coherently without running the risk of swallowing his own tongue. "Want to test those legs again?" he suggested.

What had just happened here, Hailey couldn't help wondering. One second she was certain that he was going to take her right here in the horse's stall—was she crazy or was there something incredibly sexy about that?—the next he was making noises as if he'd turned into a prim Sunday school teacher.

Had she done something wrong? Was there something in her body language that had put him off at the last moment, or was there some other reason he had backed off the way he had?

She felt so confused that her head began to ache. *Don't overthink it, just go with it and play it cool.* She'd figure all this out eventually.

So Hailey pretended to look down at her legs, as if she was passing judgment on their condition. And then she proceeded to take a guarded step forward.

And then another, a little less hesitant this time. The third step was a normal one.

"Well, whatever was wrong with them before seems to have cleared up," she informed him. Her smile was warm as she looked at him. "Thanks for catching me before I fell on my face."

"My pleasure," he told her. And then Dillon roused himself. Time for things to get back to normal, he silently insisted. "Once I get the saddles off these horses and rub them down, I'll drive you home."

Hailey was determined to make the best of the time they had left on this date and not ask any questions. "Okay, as long as you let me help." When he didn't reply, she added, "I take it that unsaddling the horses and giving them a rub down afterward is all part of riding them."

"Well yes, it is, but I can't ask you to do that."

He couldn't picture her doing anything other than standing there, looking beautiful.

"You're *not* asking me," she pointed out with a smile that went straight to his gut, even though he was trying his best to block it. "I'm volunteering to do my part," she pointed out. "Now do you want to stand here arguing about it—an argument that you're not going to win, by the way," she pointed out, "while the horses stand around, getting even more overheated? Or do you want to accept my offer to help and get to it? The faster you do, the faster you can take me home."

She had guessed right, she thought. The idea of getting her home seemed to spur him on. She tried not to let it bother her.

He shook his head. "You do have a way with words," he told her.

Confident that she had managed to win him over, Hailey flashed another grin at him, one that he found he was becoming increasingly more susceptible to, and said, "Then let's get to this, shall we?"

That grin of hers was really undoing him. Dillon found that it took everything he had not to sweep her back into his arms and kiss her again. But he was well aware of what would happen if he did that and he already knew how dangerous following that path could be. Each time he was near her like this, his immunity to her took another hit and it was becoming in dangerously low supply at this point.

Playing it safe, he took a step back, then he nodded his head and said, "All right."

Hailey found that unsaddling Delilah took a lot less time than saddling her had.

It was the rubdown that took up most of the time. Still, that was over much too soon in her estimation. Then, before she knew it, she was back in the passenger seat of Dillon's car and he was driving her home.

She told herself that she wasn't going to ask Dillon about his sudden change of heart.

As it turned out, she contained her curiosity longer than she thought she would. The drive back to her house was filled with trivial topics she introduced just to fill the air. Topics she definitely wasn't interested in and that she didn't pay any attention to even as he was talking about them.

Before she knew it, he was parking his vehicle in front of her house. And then Dillon walked her to her door.

Adding insult to injury, after refraining from kissing her goodbye, Dillon turned on his heel and began to walk away.

This time, Hailey lost the debate she was having with herself to refrain from asking questions.

"What happened, Dillon?"

She asked the question so softly, for a second, Dillon thought he had only imagined hearing her voice and only imagined hearing the question she'd asked. But then he realized that she *had* asked because, in her place, he would have wanted to know the same thing.

He would have wanted to know why.

Taking a deep breath, Dillon turned around slowly and looked at her. He was keenly aware that he owed her an explanation. But he was a private man and there were parts of himself that he couldn't share, at least not readily.

But that didn't change the fact that he *did* owe her an explanation. So he gave her one. Or at least a partial one.

"I knew that if I continued kissing you, it wouldn't stop there. And you're too nice a person to have me do that to you. I didn't want to compromise you," he added. "It wouldn't be right."

Was that it? Really? If he was telling the truth, she couldn't begin to describe the relief that washed over her. He was being noble.

But she didn't want him to be noble. She wanted

him to be himself, a man with needs. Needs that she could satisfy.

"Maybe I don't see it as being compromised," she told him gently.

"Be that as it may, I did. I do," he corrected, even as he felt himself losing ground.

"Tell you what, why don't you come inside for some coffee, or a beer," she added, thinking that might appeal to him more than just a simple cup of coffee. "And we can talk about it."

He was tempted. Very tempted, which was why taking her up on her suggestion was not a good idea. They would both regret it for different reasons. "No." He shook his head. "I'd better go."

She cocked her head, looking at him. "Why?" she asked, her voice soft and inviting. "I don't bite," she promised. "And I'd really like to understand your reasoning."

"Trust me, it's really better this way," he told her.

"Better for who?" she wanted to know. When he didn't answer her right away, she told him, "I'm open to being persuaded." Hailey smiled at him, doing her best to win him over. "And besides, I'd like to express my thanks to you for taking the time to give me a really great day I'll remember for a long time."

She could see that he was wavering so she continued to press, "You can leave at any time. I promise I won't handcuff you to anything that you can't drag in your wake. But seriously, I'd feel a lot better if you'd at least let me offer you that beer.

"It's still early," she pointed out, and then elaborated, "Too late to do anything productive, but too early just to call it a day."

He looked torn, but underneath his resolve, he knew he was slowly giving in because he really wanted to agree with her.

It was a short debate. "Okay, you win," he told her, following Hailey in.

"I'd like to think that we both win," she said as she closed the door behind them.

Chapter Fourteen

Once inside, Hailey went to the refrigerator and opened it.

"I can offer you the aforementioned beer or coffee, some tea, or I forgot I still have a partial bottle of wine from the spa's grand opening." Still holding the refrigerator door open, she turned her head to look at Dillon. "What would you like to have?"

You.

The thought flashed through his head. *Heaven help me, I'd like to have you.*

"Dillon? Did you hear me?"

Realizing he hadn't replied, he quickly answered, "Um, yes."

Hailey thought he hadn't heard her, since his answer made no sense. Not wanting to embarrass him, she gave it another shot. "Well, just to review, I can offer you two kinds of beer. Light and real beer," she said with a smile, then continued enumerating what drinks she had available. "Red wine. Coffee or tea. Those are your choices." She waited for him to pick one.

There was another choice, Dillon thought. One that neither one of them was mentioning. One that, if he remained much longer, he had a feeling would be made for him.

Dillon's eyes met hers.

She felt as if he were looking straight into her soul. And the electricity between them was so strong, she was surprised that one of them wasn't shooting off sparks from their fingertips.

Hailey took a breath, doing her best to stabilize herself.

"Tell you what," she suggested, possibly a bit too cheerfully. "Why don't I pour you a glass of wine since the bottle is already open? It would be a shame to let it go to waste."

As she talked, Hailey took out two wine glasses from the cupboard overhead. Putting them on the counter, she took the bottle out of the refrigerator, removed the cork and proceeded to pour two glasses. She brought the glasses over to the coffee table and placed one in front of Dillon as she sat down on the sofa with the other.

"To the continuing success of all your projects," she said, raising her glass in a toast. "You are all to be commended. You and your brothers have brought fresh life to this sleepy little town." She smiled warmly at him over the rim of her partially filled glass. "Thank you for all you've done."

"It was Callum's doing, really," Dillon told her quite honestly just before taking a sip of wine. He put his glass down. "He's the one with the vision," he said. "I just came along for the ride."

"You're being incredibly modest," she told him. "Don't forget, I saw what the spa building looked like *before* you worked your magic on it, transforming it into an absolute work of art in comparison." It was, she thought with pride, the first thing that new clients commented on.

"I'd hardly call it magic," Dillon protested uncomfortably.

"Maybe you wouldn't, but I would," she told him. Hailey moved closer to him without being aware of it. "You managed to take an ordinary, lackluster building and transform it into a work of art that offers its clients hope—not to mention a variety of classes to help get them achieve their goals and get into shape.

"Which reminds me," she said, her enthusiasm for her subject growing by leaps and bounds as she talked, "I've decided to add a couple of new classes to the roster. One of the classes focuses entirely on yoga and the other is a beauty treatment oriented for every inch of your body. Well, not *your* body," she corrected, her eyes traveling over him. "Your body's definitely firm enough." Realizing that she had gotten carried away, she cleared her throat. "So, what do you think?"

He didn't want to tell her what he was really thinking. That way only led to trouble. So instead, he played it safe and said, "I think that the term *spa* typically leads people to think that they're going to be lying around and getting massages and toning treatments."

"Oh, we still offer that, too," she assured him. "But the massages aren't nearly as exciting to the clients as the other things we're putting together. We're approaching wellness from all different angles." She smiled like a proud parent showing off her brand new baby. Hailey's eyes sparkled as she asked Dillon, "So what do you think?"

It wasn't up to him to approve or disapprove, but he liked her asking his opinion he thought, taking one last sip of wine, then setting down his empty glass on the coffee table. "You're the manager, not me," he told Hailey. "I'm just the guy who designed the building and oversaw the work."

"Oh, I think you did a little more than just that," she assured him. "Tell me, is your modesty a congenital thing, or is it something that you grew into gradually?"

"I was raised to think that bragging was wrong."

"And I appreciate that," she told him. "But there is a difference between bragging and accepting your due. Don't get me wrong," she added quickly, "I find your modesty charming and very sweet," she told him truthfully. "I just want you to know how good you really are, that's all.

"Sometimes," she continued, "with everything that's going on, simple things—like words of appreciation—tend to get lost and I thought you needed to hear it, at least once in a while."

Humor curved his mouth. He couldn't help thinking again how this woman was something else. "You did, did you?"

"I did," Hailey replied in all seriousness.

By this point, egged on by her enthusiasm, there was very little space left between the two of them. So little that there was only enough room to fit in a piece of paper between their bodies. A very thin piece of paper at that.

"Well then, allow me to thank you," he said, completely mesmerized by her lips with every movement they made.

"You're welcome."

Her words came out in a low sultry whisper that in any other situation might have been referred to as the beginning of a siren's song.

Dillon would have liked to have blamed it on the wine, but he had only had a couple of sips. And even if he had downed the whole glass and then the rest of what was in the bottle after that, wine wasn't nearly as potent or intoxicating as the woman sitting so close to him.

One moment he was allowing himself to be mesmerized by watching her lips move as she spoke, the very next moment he was kissing those same lips, leaving himself utterly open and vulnerable to their magic.

The last two times he had given in and kissed Hailey, he had somehow managed to be smart enough to anchor his thoughts to something, so that he could stop himself before he got too swept away.

But this time, there was no anchor to keep him from being pulled in. This time he knew he was lost the second his lips came in contact with hers. Because doing this, making love with Hailey, had been on his mind ever since he had helped her find that frog figurine at Mariana's flea market.

Ever since he'd caught himself wanting to be a frog kissed by a princess.

Almost immediately, he could all but hear his mind frantically crying out, *Mayday!* But even as it did, he sensed that it was already too late.

He knew that he didn't have a prayer of being able to bail out. At this particular time and place, he was a goner. And, heaven help him, a part of him reveled in that.

Just like that, a sense of urgency filled him. He wanted to make love with this woman before his better instincts made a reappearance and prevailed upon his sense of decency, his desire to do the right thing by everyone, including Hailey.

Maybe most of all by Hailey.

That meant walking away from her. But heaven help him, he didn't want to.

As Dillon's adrenaline rushed through his veins, making him feel like a man who was attempting to skydive without a parachute, he could feel her lips curving against his.

She was smiling.

Confused and curious, Dillon drew his head back to look at her. "What?"

"Nothing. I'm just happy," she told him simply. And then, placing a finger to his lips, she said, "No more talking."

She was right, he thought. No more talking. This wasn't the time for that. If he talked, he might just wind up stopping what he was about to do and Lord help him, he didn't want to. What he wanted to do was make love with this woman. He wanted to finish leaping out of the plane without that parachute, because even with everything that had been going on in his life—*was* going on in his life—he had *never* felt as exhilaratingly alive as he did at this very moment in time.

Dillon found himself wanting to literally devour the moment. Devour *her*. And there was nothing he could do to stop it.

Hailey could feel her head start spinning again, but this time her head felt as if it were going so fast, she could barely catch her breath.

She had come very close to giving up hope that Dillon would respond to her. Even today, there were times that she felt as if she was getting through to him, and other times she felt as if he was literally pulling away from her.

For the life of her, Hailey couldn't make sense out of his reluctance. They'd gotten along well, and when he kissed her those two other times, he hadn't been just a man taking advantage of the moment or the situation. He was right there, totally committed. And he wanted her. Not just another conquest, not just a warm body for an interlude, but *her*.

He wanted her.

Which was why, each time he drew away, throwing up that force field between them, she couldn't understand why he was doing it. Couldn't understand why this sort of rejection was happening.

But now, as they kissed over and over again with their bodies heating up, creating something between them that was theirs alone. The rest of the world just slipped away into an abyss.

Hailey had her answer.

He *wanted* her.

And for her part, she was determined he wasn't going to regret his choice.

Dillon didn't remember undressing her. Didn't remember if she had undressed him or if he had shed his own clothing in a frenzied desire to get closer to her. All he knew was that his clothes were no longer on his body and she was nude on the sofa, like a spectacular goddess right in front of him, her body primed and ready to be worshiped.

And he did.

He worshiped her with his hands, with his eyes, with his lips that eagerly passed over every single inch of her, awed as if he had been allowed access to a shrine.

Dillon couldn't get enough of her.

The more he kissed her, the more he wanted to kiss her. The more his blood heated within his body, demanding that he rush to avail himself of the final fulfillment.

But if this was going to be their one and only time together—and he had made his peace with convincing himself that it would be just this one time—he was determined that it was going to be memorable. Not for him, because it was already that for him, but for her. He never wanted her to look back at this time and feel the sting of regret eating into her soul.

So he made certain that he made love to her gently. He wanted Hailey to remember him as a kind lover. And most of all, he was determined to be a thorough lover.

With that in mind, he brought her up to the point of ecstasy not just once but several times. When her body shivered beneath him, succumbing to a climax, Dillon was quick to start building toward the next one, delivering bone-melting strokes along her body with his lips and his tongue.

With hot excitement rippling through his own body, he methodically moved down along hers, coaxing yet another explosion to reverberate throughout her moist, feverish body.

Struggling mightily to catch her breath, she bracketed his shoulders with her hands. Then she tugged on them. When he looked up at her, she managed to get one word out in a hoarse whisper.

"Together."

He understood.

Seductively sliding his body up along hers, Dillon stopped moving only when he could look into her eyes.

Again he caught her mouth, his lips slanting over hers time and again before he finally moved his knee urgently in between her legs. Silently, he got her to open for him.

Then, weaving a necklace of lingering hot kisses along the top of her breasts and throat, Dillon moved up just a little higher until his eyes were on hers.

And then, with one movement of his hips, he entered her and they became one palpitating unit, driven by one desire: to set the night on fire.

His heart pounding in his chest, Dillon still managed to keep himself in check and move slowly at first.

But as the tempo in his head increased, he began to move faster, and then faster still.

Hailey found that she had somehow managed to feel the same rhythm that was driving him. It propelled her on. She was mimicking each of his movements, recreating them so that the need increased a little more each time she moved her hips against his.

She could hardly contain herself.

They raced one another to the very top of the highest peak before them and then, just for the tiniest of moments, they flew, wrapped up in ecstasy, reveling in the powerful feeling that had seized them, before they slowly began to descend, still joined, still one with the moment and each other.

The euphoria of the afterglow lingered and they held onto one another—and it—for as long as they were able, each loath to surrender to reality and to the world that was waiting to claim them back.

And when it was all over, Dillon lay there on the sofa, feeling her heart beating hard against his.

Part of him was still floating, still wrapped in a delicious, impenetrable mist. But another part of him felt as if perhaps he needed to apologize for letting things go this far when he didn't have the right to allow it to get this out of hand.

Because in doing it, he had made silent promises that he was not at liberty to keep.

He felt Hailey stirring beneath him as reality took on length and breadth. He could have sworn that the room had grown colder.

"I'm sorry," Dillon said, shifting in order to give Hailey as much space as he could on the sofa. It wasn't much.

She took his apology at face value. Dillon was just apologizing for crowding her on the sofa. Granted it wasn't exactly the best place for this to have happened, she silently acknowledged, but even so, it had still been beyond wonderful.

"That's all right," Hailey assured him. "The sofa wasn't built for comfort, not when it comes to this sort of thing, anyway," she allowed with a soft, gentle laugh. "But that's why beds were invented," she told him with a wink.

The next moment, she was sitting up and then wiggling off the sofa to stand before him in what he could only describe as breathtaking magnificence.

Taking Dillon's hand, she drew him off the sofa, as well.

"Why don't we put my theory to the test?" Hailey suggested.

He wasn't following her. "Theory?"

"About beds and sofas. If this was your place, we'd need a compass right about now to get to your bedroom, but my bedroom's just down the hall," she told him. Tugging on his hand, she led the way.

It didn't escape her attention that he paused to grab his slacks—and his cell phone—but she was feeling far too euphoric at the moment to let it bother her.

After all, he seemed to pride himself for being perpetually on call. She accepted it as being part of who he was.

Chapter Fifteen

Feeling blissfully fulfilled, Hailey woke up the next morning with a smile on her face.

Last night had been far and away the most wonderful night of her life. Dillon turned out to be everything she could have possibly asked for in a lover—and more. They wound up making love two more times last night. Each and every time they had, Dillon was even more of a considerate, generous lover than he had been the time before.

The last time they made love, Hailey almost cried. She was that touched by him, that thrilled. Finally too spent to do anything but smile up at Dillon, she fell asleep curled up in his arms.

When she opened her eyes this morning, she was surprised to find that sometime during what was left of the night, Dillon had pulled away from her. As she looked at him now, it was obvious that he had gone to sleep as far over on his side of the queen-sized bed as possible.

It was probably just a sleeping habit of his, she told herself. Some people just needed space in order to fall asleep and they couldn't do it if they felt confined or crowded.

Don't make a big deal out of it. Focus on the fact that Dillon made love with you three times, not that he seems to like to sleep unencumbered.

She was close to convincing herself when her heart nearly stopped as Dillon's eyes suddenly flew open. Her gentle, wonderful lover was looking at her as if she was some sort of invader. Or, at the very least, someone he would have rather not found lying next to him first thing in the morning.

Don't take it personally, Hailey. Maybe your Frog Prince isn't a morning person.

Determined to push past the painfully uneasy feeling that was beginning to form in the pit of her stomach, Hailey forced a smile to her lips as she looked at him.

"So," she asked softly, "how did you sleep?"

"I slept okay." His answer was short, abrupt, his voice distant.

Hailey could have sworn she almost felt the

walls of his fortress resurrecting themselves around Dillon right in front of her eyes. He was regretting what had happened, she thought. She could sense it.

But she *knew* he had enjoyed himself, she silently insisted. Why was he doing this now? Why was he acting as if he didn't care one way or another? Why wouldn't he allow himself to open up to her?

Her heart sank. What did she have to do to get through to him and get him to trust her?

Well, crowding him wasn't going to do it, she thought. With effort, she tried to get herself to back off.

Momentarily at a loss as to how to move forward, Hailey said the first thing that came into her mind. When in doubt, offer food.

"Would you like some breakfast, Dillon?" she asked. "I can—"

"Would you mind if I showered first?" he asked, sitting up in bed and shifting away from her.

She felt as if an arrow had pierced her heart. Did Dillon want to get the scent of her, of their lovemaking, off his body?

Stop it. You're going to make yourself crazy.

Hailey deliberately forced another smile to her lips and said in as cheerful a voice as she could muster, "Sure, go ahead. The bathroom's right over—"

She didn't get a chance to finish. Taking the blanket that was at the foot of her bed, Dillon secured it around his waist. With it draped over his body, he walked into the bathroom.

Maybe he'd feel better once he'd showered, she consoled herself. The man who had made love to her last night couldn't have just vanished without a trace. Not completely. Maybe he just needed a few minutes to himself so he could evaluate what he'd done, what had happened between them.

Maybe—

The sound of the running water in the shower was suddenly interrupted by the insistent beeping of a cell phone. Pulling herself together, Hailey looked around for her phone. Belatedly, she remembered that it was still in her purse. And she'd left her purse on the living room floor.

The sound couldn't have carried this far, she reasoned.

But there it was again, that insistent beeping sound, demanding attention.

Where—?

And then she remembered. Dillon had brought his cell phone, along with his slacks, into her bedroom when they came in here last night.

There it was again. The jarring noise scissored its way under her skin. It didn't sound as if whoever was calling was about to give up.

Given how early it was, she decided that Dillon was probably missing a call from one of his brothers. Knowing how dedicated he was to their projects, Hailey went looking for the cell.

He was probably going to use this call as an excuse to beat a hasty retreat once he came out of her bathroom, but she couldn't very well ignore the call. The more she thought about it, the more she felt that it was probably something important.

Resigned, she began her search, trying to determine where Dillon had dropped his phone.

The annoying beeping sound stopped. The caller apparently had finally given up, she thought. And then she saw it. His phone was lying face down on her floor. Dillon must have accidentally kicked it as he made his way into her shower because the phone was partially under her bed with only an end peeking out.

She picked up the phone, went to place it on the nightstand. But the contact and movement had caused the last series of unviewed texts to pop up on the screen.

The texts were all from the same person. Someone named Julie. The last text was written all in capitals.

WHEN ARE YOU COMING HOME????

Hailey didn't remember sitting down, but she must have. Her knees suddenly gave out and she found herself sinking back onto her bed.

She felt as if she had just been kicked in her stomach.

Julie.

The name seemed to dance in front of her eyes, mocking her.

Julie? Who was Julie?

Was Dillon already involved with someone else? Worse, was he *married*?

Was *that* the reason he had kept her at arm's length—when he remembered his marital status? Because he certainly hadn't acted like he was married last night.

She felt tears gathering in her eyes and she wiped them away. If Dillon was married, then why hadn't he *told* her?

She was a great believer in privacy. Usually. But unable to help herself, she scrolled down through the messages that were available to her, the ones that had been sent and hadn't been looked at yet. She couldn't remember even hearing the phone beeping before now, but then, they had been rather busy last night, oblivious to everything else except each other.

The memory of that didn't console her now. It made her feel as if she had been underhanded. Not as underhanded as Dillon, but hey, they couldn't all be in his league, she thought, a stab of bitterness lancing right into her heart.

Again, she berated herself for reading his private messages like this. But in her defense, she was trying to find something—*anything*—to prove that she was wrong, that this wasn't what it looked like.

But when the same message kept popping up all four times in progressively bigger text, she knew that this *had* to be exactly what it looked like. This Julie woman appeared to have far more of a claim on Dillon than Hailey did.

Hailey knew she had to be right because why else would he have kept this woman a secret from her?

Feeling progressively sicker, she desperately wanted to run away. She wanted to hide from this awful pain that was carving up her insides.

But damn it, this was *her* house, not his. If anyone needed to leave because of this awful discovery, it was Dillon.

Grabbing a robe from her closet, Hailey had just managed to shrug into it to cover herself and tied the sash at her waist when Dillon walked out. Bare-chested and barefoot, he was only wearing his slacks. His hair was wet from the shower.

Without saying a word to him, she got up and shoved his phone into his hand.

Dillon looked down at the screen. Seeing the row of texts, one after the other, he quickly retreated back into the bathroom without saying a word.

Feeling so awful that she found herself fighting

a very strong, very real urge to throw up, Hailey sat back down on her bed, struggling to get a grip on herself.

She wasn't going to cry, she wasn't, she silently ordered herself. Hailey took in a couple of deep breaths, trying very hard not to dissolve in tears.

When Dillon came out again, she was just going to tell him that she wasn't feeling well and would he mind leaving? Permanently?

Hailey fisted her hands beside her. She just couldn't deal with this right now, she couldn't.

But just as she couldn't stop the tears that welled up in her eyes, she couldn't lie or pretend that none of this was happening. She had just made love to a married man—or to a man who might as well be married. He was definitely involved with someone, which to her was the same thing.

The bottom line was she had made love with someone who hadn't been honest with her. And to her, dishonesty was just about the worst.

Hailey jumped when the bathroom door suddenly opened. She swung around just in time to look Dillon straight in the eye.

"Who is Julie and why is she asking you to come home?" Hailey asked him in a shaky voice.

Startled, Dillon looked at her. "You read my texts?" he asked, surprised.

"That's not the important part here," she informed him in a strained, angry voice. "Who is Julie?" she asked again.

"It's not what you think," Dillon began, searching for words that wouldn't escalate what already felt like a totally volatile disaster about to explode.

"I don't *know* what to think," Hailey cried, exasperated. "Because you keep shutting me out. Every time I think we've made a little progress, every time it looks like we've taken one step forward, you do something to push me back not one step but two. I'm through with you keeping things to yourself," she declared, then, out of patience, she demanded, "Is Julie your wife?"

Dillon looked at her, stunned. "No, Julie's not my wife," he answered. "She is—"

He was talking too slow, Hailey thought angrily. She wanted to jump down his throat and physically drag all his words out.

"She's what, Dillon?" Hailey cried, frustrated. "Your girlfriend?"

His blue eyes turning darker, he finally replied, "Julie's my daughter."

Hailey felt as if all the air had just been pumped out of her lungs. For a second, her head reeling, she was totally speechless and could only stare at Dillon, wide-eyed.

"Your daughter," she finally said, repeating the words numbly. The import of what Dillon had just said hit her right between the eyes. "Oh, my Lord, I'm a home-wrecker," she cried.

"No," Dillon firmly insisted. "You're not a home-wrecker, Hailey."

He could see that she wasn't convinced. That was when Dillon did something he never did. He forced himself to open up, at least a little, about his private life.

"There is no home to wreck, Hailey," Dillon told her quietly.

"But your daughter—" she protested.

"Is the product of a teenage romance." He could see that she was waiting for more so he forced himself to keep talking. "When I found out that my girl-friend, Maura, was pregnant, I wanted to step up and do the right thing. I told her that I'd marry her. Hell, I *wanted* to marry her."

"So what happened?" Hailey wanted to know. Heaven knew that if he had offered to marry *her*, to give their child a father as well as his name, *she* certainly wouldn't have hesitated saying yes to him. She would have said it so fast his head would have spun.

She found herself not liking this Maura person

because she could see that the woman had obviously hurt Dillon.

"*She* didn't want to marry me. I thought that maybe she was being stubborn, that she was embarrassed to be in this condition and didn't want me to feel I *had* to marry her.

"But as it turned out, she really wasn't in love with me. She didn't want to get married just because it was the *right* thing to do, or just to give her baby a last name." He smiled ruefully, remembering the scene as if it had been yesterday. "She told me that her baby would have a last name. *Her* last name."

"I don't think I understand," Hailey confessed.

Though it was painful for him, Dillon continued telling her the story. "For whatever reason, Maura decided to keep me from having any contact with Julie. She disappeared right after she had the baby. I tried to keep track of her and the baby because, well, after all, Julie was my responsibility, my *child*.

"I finally managed to track her down a couple of years ago and found that Maura had relocated not all that far away from where I lived. As it turned out, she had gone on to marry someone she did love." He smiled sadly. "As for Julie, she turned out to be a very headstrong, stubborn girl. She got it into her head to look into finding me on her own. The internet can be a very helpful tool if you're as resourceful as Julie is."

There was no missing the pride in Dillon's voice, Hailey thought. He really was a decent human being, she decided, relieved.

"It took some time, but Julie managed to track me down. She's a stubborn girl. I guess she takes after me," he said with a smile. "Once she did, she got in contact with me behind Maura's back. We started exchanging cards and letters. That went on for two years and then she asked if she could see me. By then Callum had gotten involved with building up Rambling Rose and we were all about to relocate. He was counting on me for my help, so I told Julie that we would get together once I got back to Fort Lauderdale. She accepted it at first. Julie's resourceful and bright, but she is still a twelve-year-old girl and they tend to be impatient at that age. I suppose that's the reason she sent all those texts to me. She became impatient."

Hailey ached for the little girl, thinking how she had to feel, finally finding her father and not being able to get together with him. "So what are you going to do?" she wanted to know.

"I haven't figured it out yet," Dillon admitted. "The one thing I do plan to do is see Julie. She deserves a father, her *real* father, and I don't plan on abandoning her for a second time now that we've made contact of a sort. I've already missed too much of her life. I don't intend to miss the rest of it."

"And what about Julie's mother? You said she wouldn't let you see Julie. What if she doesn't change her mind?" Hailey asked. What she didn't add was that Dillon had said Maura had turned him down when he asked to marry her and then had married someone else. That had to have hurt Dillon, she thought. Maura had been his first love. Could he wind up changing his mind about her if she acted as if she regretted her initial decision?

As if reading her mind, Dillon told her, "Anything between Maura and me has long since died. But that doesn't change the fact that I *am* Julie's dad and Julie wants a chance to get to know me. Maura is just going to have to find a way to deal with it," he said with finality. "I guess," Dillon continued after a moment, "getting kicked in the teeth that way at seventeen permanently destroyed any tendency I might have had to view romance with any sort of a positive, rosy attitude."

She knew what he was telling her. That he wasn't able to open himself up and care for her the way she wanted him to because he'd been permanently scarred at a young age. She fought the urge to tell him that *she* wasn't like Maura, but she sensed that he had already opened himself up far more than he had intended to and that she shouldn't push it. So she refrained.

Instead she said, "Not *everyone* is like Maura."

"No," Dillon agreed, "they're not. But putting myself out there and possibly setting myself up for a fall is just too painful. Besides, since Julie is in Fort Lauderdale, my place is there if I ever hope to form any sort of relationship with my daughter."

He took a deep breath and looked directly into Hailey's eyes. "What I'm trying to say is that I'm not free to start anything that would lead to a relationship between us. I can't promise you that I'm going to stick around," he said flatly. Dillon took her hands in his. "As a matter of fact, I can probably promise you the exact opposite." He looked at Hailey seriously. "I'm not about to give up on Julie."

"I wouldn't ask you to," Hailey replied in total sincerity.

Dillon knew she thought she meant that, but things had a habit of changing. There was a time he could have sworn that Maura loved him, but he had turned out to be wrong.

"That's what you say now," Dillon began, "but—"

Hailey placed her finger to his lips, stopping him before he could say anything further. "Why don't we just take this one day at a time and see where it leads?" she suggested.

In his heart, he welcomed that because he really didn't want to just walk away from Hailey. Not while they could still see each other. But he did have his doubts about the arrangement.

"You'd be okay with that?" Dillon asked her in surprise.

"Yes," she answered with a smile. "Look, I know we're in Texas, but I'm not about to throw a lasso over you and hog-tie you so you can't get away. Listen," she continued, "I wouldn't want you if you were uncomfortable being in this relationship just as you wouldn't want me if I was uncomfortable." Then she added what she felt was the clinching argument. "Just as you let Maura go because she said she wasn't comfortable being in a relationship with you."

He looked at her for a long moment. Hailey was making a valid point and it was definitely something for him to think about. But he still knew in the back of his mind that he was going to have trouble putting his fears to rest. Like the very real fear that, if he suddenly decided to stay and opened up his heart to Hailey, something might still happen to make her abruptly change her mind and terminate any sort of relationship that was growing between them.

Once burnt, twice leery...

Still, for now, Dillon felt himself relenting... just a little.

"Like you said, one step at a time," he replied, nodding his head.

Last night had shown her that Dillon knew exactly how to set her world on fire. If he couldn't just leap headlong into a relationship with her without looking back, she was just going to have to find a way to live with that, Hailey told herself.

Live with it and hope for the best. She was going to show Dillon how steadfast she could be and, more importantly, that she was nothing at all like the woman who had crippled his heart.

Chapter Sixteen

Dillon and Hailey continued seeing one another during any free time they could find and stitch together. It was a tall order between his construction projects and her work at the spa. The latter was currently deemed to be another success for Callum and the company, but that didn't mean she had the luxury of dropping the ball either figuratively *or* literally. She worked exceeding hard, which made any free time she spent with Dillon that much more precious and sweet.

However, whenever they did find small islands of time to spend together, Hailey couldn't shake the feeling that they weren't really alone. The specter of Maura and Dillon's failed romance was always there with them in the background, like a nebulous prophesy of doom.

And then, after what had been a promising start, their relationship stalled like a manual transmission stuck in second gear.

Try as she might, Hailey couldn't seem to convince Dillon to loosen up and really take a chance on them.

Added to that was another concurrent problem. Maura continued to throw a wrench into any headway their relationship could have made by refusing to budge on the subject of Julie. The woman was determined that Julie just wouldn't have any sort of a relationship with Dillon.

Ever.

All this made Dillion leery of beginning a new romance. The only time he'd fallen in love, he'd made a mess of things. How could he expect a different result now?

He hadn't expected his twelve-year-old daughter to indirectly provide a solution by finding a way to work around every roadblock Maura put in their path.

For more than two years Maura kept the cards, letters and gifts that he had sent from reaching Julie. For reasons that would forever remain a mystery to him, Maura didn't destroy them. Instead, she locked them up in a box she kept hidden in the back of her bedroom closet.

And then, as fate would have it, when Maura went into the hospital for an appendectomy, Julie accidentally came across a letter he had mailed to her while her babysitter was in the other room. Since it was obviously addressed to her, Julie read it. Surprised, stunned and exceedingly happy that her father cared enough to write to her, he found out that Julie became convinced that there had to be more letters she hadn't seen. A relentless search through her mother's things led her to find the other letters that Maura had hidden.

When he received that first letter from his daughter, he couldn't begin to describe the immense joy he experienced. Although he didn't approve of deception, he felt this was the only way that he and his daughter could get to know one another so he sent the girl money and told her how to set up a postal box in a local office supply store, so that he could send his letters to her there.

The hope was that until Maura could be convinced to allow him to meet their daughter face-to-face, they would continue making contact this way. He knew he could take this to court and fight for visitation rights, but he didn't want an all out war with Maura because he didn't want Julie caught in the middle. It would only hurt her. But neither did he want Julie to feel that he was giving up on her, so he kept writing to the girl.

But he never gave up trying to convince Maura to let him into Julie's life.

Once she was aware of what was going on, Hailey encouraged him to keep working on Maura.

"No luck?" Hailey asked after she watched Dillon terminate yet another phone call to the girl's mother.

Dillon shook his head, frustrated. "She still refuses to let me see Julie, or even talk to her. If she ever realized that Julie and I were communicating, she'd probably disappear with the girl just to spite me. I'd wind up never hearing from Julie again."

Hailey ached for him and the pain she knew he had to be going through.

"Maura can't just take off like that," Hailey said, trying to make him feel better. "You said she was married, right? Her husband has a job, doesn't he?" she asked.

Dillon knew where she was going with this, but he also knew that Hailey wasn't totally aware of the whole situation.

"He does," Dillon answered. "But from what I gather from the things she did tell me, her husband has no spine. That means that he does *every-*

thing Maura wants in order to keep her happy and maintain peace."

The woman sounded like some sort of dragon lady, and in Hailey's opinion, Dillon had definitely dodged a bullet when Maura had turned down his proposal almost thirteen years ago.

Not wanting to sound critical, she kept that to herself. But she did say something that occurred to her just now. "If she keeps refusing to let you even meet Julie and you're worried that they might just vanish if you so much as push Maura to let you see the girl, then why are you still considering moving to Florida?"

He knew she probably thought he was hitting his head against a wall and maybe he was. But he shrugged helplessly, saying, "On the outside chance that I could wear her down eventually."

Because it was her habit, Hailey tried to see the situation in the best possible light. This time, that *best* light was about Dillon's attitude.

"I guess there is a bit of an optimist in you, after all," she said, smiling at him.

"Maybe so, but that optimist is fading pretty fast," he told her.

Even so, Hailey was determined to fan that flame and keep it alive until it could burn on its own. She felt it was also the only chance for them to have any future together.

"If you give up now, you'll never get to see your daughter and that's that," she told him. "But if you keep on trying to get through to Maura, to get her to change her mind, you still have a chance."

Dillon shook his head, amazed. "You really believe that?"

"With my whole heart and soul," she answered with feeling. She put her hand on his shoulder. "You have nothing to lose if you keep trying and everything to lose if you don't."

He laughed, but it wasn't at her. He was reacting to the warmth her words generated. "Do you get these sayings off bumper stickers, or from fortune cookies?"

"From life," she answered, then smiled. "Like I said when I first met you, you could stand to take part in one of my spa sessions."

He slipped his arm around her, pulling her in closer so he could kiss her. Heaven help him, she did make him feel better, even though he didn't quite share her overall outlook, or her peppy sayings. It was the way Hailey said them—and the fact that he needed to have something to hold on to—that gave him a lifeline.

Despite everything he had done to try to discourage Hailey, she continued to maintain her optimism—and to give him hope. He was lucky to have her in his life. "Want to see her picture?" he asked.

"I'd love to."

Dillon took out his wallet and took out a small snapshot. "I made a print of it in case I ever lose my phone."

She loved hearing the pride in his voice. "She's adorable," Hailey told him.

"Yeah," he paused to look at it a moment longer, "I think so, too."

Dillon had just finished going over the final layout for his construction company's next joint project: Provisions, the restaurant that was going to be a joint venture run by his triplet sisters, Ashley, Nicole and Megan, when his cell phone rang. Involved in the review, he didn't hear it at first. When he did, he put down his pencil next to the notes he'd been making.

He had made plans to see Hailey this evening— a rare midweek treat because they were both so busy the last few days—and he thought it was Hailey calling with a possible last-minute change in plans.

"Hi, honey," Dillon said, mechanically swiping open his phone while still looking over the restaurant's layout.

The sharp voice on the other end of the call

took him completely by surprise. Hearing it, Dillon nearly dropped his phone.

"Don't you *honey* me, damn it!" the woman shouted.

"Maura?" It wasn't really a question. Her voice, filled with anger, drilled itself into his head.

Why was she calling him out of the blue like this? And what on earth could he have possibly done to upset her so much?

"Of course it's me!" Maura snapped, her voice shrill. "Don't act like you didn't expect to hear from me."

"I didn't," he told her honestly. "Why are you calling?" he asked, a little frustrated by her tone.

"Like you don't know," she accused.

Dillon sighed. She couldn't have picked a worse time to call. "Maura, I don't have time for games today. I've got a lot on my plate."

"Oh, you do, do you?" she asked in a mocking voice. "Does one of those *things* on your plate include picking up Julie from the airport?" Maura's voice rose as she shouted at him.

"What are you talking about?" he asked when he was able to get a word in edgewise.

"Don't play dumb, Dillon. You know exactly what I'm talking about!" Practically beside herself, Maura was almost screeching at this point.

They were going around in circles, Dillon

thought wearily. It was something he had learned that Maura had quite an aptitude for.

"Why don't you pretend I don't," he told her.

She didn't seem to hear him. "You're responsible for this!" she accused. "Filling Julie's head with a bunch of nonsense, turning her against Bill!" she cried, referring to her husband, Julie's stepfather.

Dillon was struggling to piece things together from the bits of information he was able to glean from her ranting. Why would Maura even think that? "You know I wouldn't do that."

"Right, because you're such an honorable man," the woman on the other end mocked.

Dillon thought that she sounded as if she was growing more and more angry. But beneath the anger, he detected a ripple of fear. Had something happened to Julie?

He needed to cut through all this angry rhetoric so he could find out just why Maura was calling and hurling these accusations at him.

"Maura, you're not making any sense. Now you start telling me what this is all about," he told her.

And then, to Dillon's surprise, the woman on the other end broke down and started to cry. "Julie. It's about Julie," she sobbed.

Fear was suddenly twisting a knife in his gut, carving him up. Maura sounded as if she was falling apart. Maura *never* fell apart. She prided herself on that. Something awful had to have happened to their daughter.

He struggled to remain calm. To *sound* calm. "What about Julie?" he asked, even as his breath was backing up in his throat.

"She's run away from home!"

"Run away?" he repeated. That didn't make any sense to him. Julie was far too stable to do something like that. "Are you sure? Maybe she's just at one of her friends' houses."

"Of course I'm sure!" Maura shouted at him. "Don't you think I've already called all of her friends? She's not there. She's not anywhere," Maura sobbed helplessly. "She's run away, I tell you! To see *you*," she accused.

Maura's mind was conjuring things up now, he thought. He did his best to reason with her and calm her down. "Maura, you're in Florida. I'm halfway across the country in Texas. I really don't think that—"

"She left me a note," Maura cried, cutting in. "She said that since I wouldn't let you come to see her, she was going to go to see you and that I couldn't do anything to stop her!" She was sobbing again. "This is all your fault!" she accused again.

Stunned, Dillon's mind dragged up half a dozen scenarios all involving runaways, none of them good. He needed to find her, he thought, trying not to panic. "Did you call the police?"

"I didn't," she bit off. "I called you. But if you don't bring Julie back the second you find her, I will call them and tell them that you kidnapped my daughter! See if you can talk your way out of that!"

"Maura, calm down!" Dillon said loudly, hoping to get some order into the discussion. "I didn't kidnap Julie. *I don't have her,*" he said emphatically. "But I will find her," he promised. Taking a breath, he tried to think. "When was the last time you saw her?"

"This morning—no, last night," she realized. "I had an early meeting with my boss this morning, so I left before she went to school. I didn't see her."

"You left her alone?" he asked incredulously.

"No, of course not. Bill was still home—and don't try to turn things around to blame me! You're the guilty one here!" she cried.

Trying to make Maura see things from his side was frustrating, but she was right—he needed to find Julie before something happened to her. So Dillon continued asking Maura questions, hoping he could get to the bottom of this and figure out if Julie really had run away from home to see him. And somehow, at least for old times sake, he needed to find a way to help Maura calm down.

Chapter Seventeen

He was late, Hailey thought.

She had taken part of the day off because Dillon had told her he wanted to see her. But he was already over an hour late and she was getting antsy. There was no sign of him.

Where was he?

She had reached for her phone several times now, wanting to call him, but she'd refrained each time. She really didn't want Dillon to feel as if she was crowding him. The man didn't need that right now.

She knew that Dillon was worried about his daughter who had been missing since yesterday, and more than anything, she wished she knew what to do in order to help him find her—that is if the girl really had run away the way her mother said she had.

There was the very real possibility that Maura was blowing all this way out of proportion. Secretly Hailey was still holding out hope that the girl had decided to just go to one of her friends' houses to either teach her mother a lesson or just get some time away from her mother who seemed like she could be somewhat overbearing.

Piecing things together from just one side of the conversation as she listened to Dillon attempt to talk to Maura, Julie's mother was apparently bent on making father and daughter pay in their separate ways for daring to forge a relationship behind her back. To Hailey, the woman came off sounding extremely insecure.

Just as Hailey was about to start pacing the floor, she heard the doorbell ring. She instantly snapped to attention and ran out of the kitchen.

Throwing the door open, she cried, "I was beginning to really get worried that you—"

The rest of her sentence died, unspoken, on her lips when she saw who was on the other side.

It wasn't Dillon standing in her doorway, it was a young girl with straight dirty blond hair and bright blue eyes. Caught completely by surprise, Hailey blinked, and then looked at the girl again, this time a little more closely.

Even if she hadn't seen a picture, she would have known her, anyway. "Julie?"

It was more of a greeting than a question. The moment she said the girl's name, she knew she was right. The angry-looking girl on her doorstep looked like a young female version of Dillon.

Julie raised her chin as if she was expecting some sort of challenge from the woman who had opened the door. In a voice that sounded entirely too grown up, the girl asked, "Is Dillon Fortune here? I can't find him."

Hailey couldn't help wondering how Julie had gotten her address—had Dillon given it to her, thinking that another woman might make the girl somehow feel safe if she ever decided to come here?

That had to be it, she decided. Either that or he had mentioned her by name as a friend and the resourceful little girl had looked her up when she didn't find her father at his place. There was time enough to delve into that later. Right now, there were more pressing things to address. Like how she had gotten here.

"No," Hailey answered the girl, "but I'm expecting him any minute now. C'mon in," she invited, opening the door as wide as she could. When Julie made no effort to budge, Hailey added, "Please."

"Okay," Julie finally grudgingly agreed, walking in with some reluctance. "But you *are* expecting him here, right?"

"Actually, he should already be here," Hailey told Dillon's daughter.

She looked over the girl's shoulder, expecting to see whoever had accompanied Julie here from Fort Lauderdale. But there was no one with the girl nor did she look as if she was waiting for someone to catch up to her, like a person who was still parking a car perhaps.

This was really unusual, Hailey thought.

She had to ask. "Did you come all this way by yourself?" Hailey wanted to know, finally closing the door behind her.

Julie straightened her shoulders. "I used my mother's credit card. What of it?" Her tone sounded as if she was ready for a fight.

"Nothing," Hailey told the girl mildly. "You're just a little young to be traveling all that way by yourself," she observed.

Julie's eyes narrowed into small lethal laser beams. Hailey could have sworn the girl's nostrils flared, as well.

"I'm twelve," Julie declared as if that totally negated any question of her being too young to make the trip. "I just said my mother was sending me to stay with my father. Nobody asked any questions," she said proudly.

It wasn't her place to say anything about lying, Hailey thought. She didn't want to antagonize Dillon's daughter. Instead, she asked, "Does your mother know you're here?" she asked, even though she knew the answer to that was a resounding no. She wanted to see what the girl had to say in response.

The answer was typical of a preteen. "She took away my phone, so it's her own fault she can't find me. Besides, my mother doesn't care about anyone but herself," Julie declared dismissively.

Hailey caught herself feeling sorry for both mother and daughter trapped in this dance with no music. "I happen to know that's not true, Julie. Your mother is very worried about you."

Julie sniffed and tossed her head, sending her hair flying over her shoulder. "How would you know? Did she tell you?"

"No, but she told your father," Hailey said. "Your mother called yesterday looking for you and she was frantic."

Restless, Julie began roaming around the living

room and kitchen. Her eyes darted back and forth as she took in every single detail. When it came to Hailey's assessment of her mother's reaction, Julie shrugged dismissively. Instead, she looked at Hailey more closely, as if she was passing judgment on her.

Growing wary, Hailey observed Julie frowning at her. There was an edge in the girl's voice as she asked, "Are you my father's girlfriend?"

She hoped that was what he thought. But she knew better than to reach that conclusion before anything had been said. And she definitely didn't want to risk alienating Julie.

"You're going to have to ask your father that. What I can tell you is that your dad's been beside himself ever since your mother called to tell him that you ran away. He's been calling everyone he knows back in Fort Lauderdale, asking them to try to find you."

Suddenly, the belligerent preteen vanished, replaced by a hopeful little girl who looked at her with wide eyes. "He has?"

Hailey nodded. There wasn't so much as a hint of a smile on her lips. "The last I heard, he was trying to hire a reputable private detective to look for you."

"But I'm here," Julie protested, spreading her hands wide.

Hailey took her cell phone out. "And that's what I'm going to tell him the second I reach your father," she said, beginning to input Dillon's phone number. She paused a second to smile at Julie, relieved that the girl had turned up unharmed. "He's going to really be thrilled to see you."

For a moment, Julie looked undecided and torn, as if she really wanted to believe what Hailey was telling her, but at the same time, she didn't know if she could.

"If that's true, then why didn't he come to see me? I must have asked him to more than a dozen times," Julie told her.

From the tone she used, Hailey could tell that the girl had a giant chip on her shoulder. She knew that if she sounded as if she was lecturing Julie, that would just exacerbate the situation, not alleviate it. She chose her words carefully, watching Julie's face.

"Because your mother told him she didn't want your dad coming to see you. She was afraid that would wind up disrupting your life."

Julie shook her head, looking as if she didn't understand. "But he's my dad," she cried. "He should have come anyway, no matter what my mother said. Didn't he want to see me?"

Hailey looked into the girl's eyes. Empathy ran all through her. Julie was hurting and she did what she could to reassure her.

"You know the answer to that," she told Julie. "More than anything. But sometimes, it's better to go slowly than just barge straight in. Trust me," she assured the girl.

"But—"

After dialing and redialing several times, just to have her calls go to voice mail, Hailey finally heard the phone being picked up on the other end.

Dillon started talking immediately without giving her a chance to say a word.

"Look, Hailey, I know I said I'd be over, but I can't right now. Something's come up and—"

"Dillon," Hailey blurted, cutting him off. "She's here. Julie's here."

"What?" Dillon asked. What was she telling him? It was as if the words weren't registering in his brain. All he knew was that he was waiting for a call he had placed to a detective agency to come through.

"Julie's here," Hailey told him again, not bothering to curb her excitement. After having him go through hell, worried sick about his daughter, she was thrilled to be able to give him some good news. The *best* news, really, she thought.

Numb, Dillon was almost afraid of jumping to a conclusion that might lead to disappointment. "Where's here?" he asked uncertainly.

"My house," Hailey answered. "Julie's here at my house."

Stunned, Dillon could only ask, "When?"

"Just now," she answered happily. "Why don't you—" the call suddenly went dead "—come over?" Hailey concluded, even though she knew Dillon couldn't hear her anymore.

Putting her cell phone away, she looked at Julie.

"He's on his way," she told the girl, then felt that in all likelihood, a warning was in order. "Your dad might be kind of angry and he might yell when he gets here, but you need to keep in mind that he really doesn't mean it. You gave him quite a scare by running off like that. Remember, your dad really loves you."

Julie looked at her uncertainly, clearly torn again. "He said that?"

This wasn't the time to qualify her statement by saying that Dillon hadn't said those exact words, but that was what he meant. If she said that, Julie would discount anything she would have to say after that. No, now was the time for reassurances, Hailey silently told herself.

With that, she told the girl, "Yes. Yes, he did."

For her trouble, she saw an incredibly wide smile bloom on the girl's face.

"Really?" Julie asked again, her eyes shining as she waited to get the same answer.

"Really," Hailey repeated.

Julie paused for a moment, as if she was digesting everything very slowly and with relish. And then she looked at Hailey, curious.

"How did you meet my father?" she wanted to know.

That one was easy to field. "He renovated the spa that I manage."

"When did he—"

Whatever the girl was about to ask was going to have to wait because just then the doorbell rang. Julie's head practically spun as she looked toward her front door.

"That's probably your father now," Hailey told her as she headed for the door.

Julie was right behind her, her eyes never leaving the entrance.

A sudden surge of nerves had her looking toward Hailey for guidance.

"What do I say?" Julie asked, fighting back a wave of panic.

"Hi, Dad would be a good start," Hailey said as she opened the door.

Any other exchanges or warnings were all put on hold because Dillon suddenly hurried inside. The second he saw her, he swept his daughter into his arms, hugging her to him as relief overwhelmed him. It was also the very first time he had ever been able to hug her and he wasn't about to let go, not for a while.

He spun her around and then, finally, before he was completely overcome with emotion, he set her back down again.

"Are you all right?" he asked anxiously.

"I'm okay," Julie cried, her own young voice filled with emotion.

Dillon took a deep breath, attempting to distance himself from all the emotions that were swirling through him right now. "What were you thinking, running away like that?"

"I was thinking that I wanted to see you and Mom wouldn't let me. She wouldn't even let me talk to her about it," Julie cried.

Her eyes were shining with tears and it was obvious that she expected him to understand.

He struggled to be the father she needed and

made another attempt to try to discipline her. "But—"

This was a very fragile situation, Hailey thought. One misstep on his part and things could really go badly for him while he was trying to establish this shaky relationship. She knew she should keep out of this, but she couldn't.

"That doesn't matter right now," she told Dillon. "What matters is that she's your daughter and she's here and you both love each other. You can work out the rest of that later," Hailey told both father and daughter. "Right now all you really need to do is get acquainted."

"No," Dillon answered, "We can do that on the plane when we take Julie back. Right now," he told his daughter, "I need to call your mother and keep her from having a nervous breakdown."

Julie looked completely unmoved when he mentioned her mother. She waved her hand dismissively. "She doesn't care."

"Oh, yes, she does," Dillon insisted. "Whatever is going down between your mother and me, make no mistake about that. She loves you very much and she deserves to know that nothing happened to you," he told his daughter. He began to dial Maura's number. "How did you wind up here, anyway?" he wanted to know. She had obviously flown here from Florida and airplane tickets weren't exactly going for a song.

"I paid for it," she proudly informed him as he heard the cell phone begin to ring.

"How?" he pressed, still dubious about what she was telling him.

"I've been saving my allowance for something important for a long time now," Julie announced.

This being-a-dad thing was going to take some getting used to, he thought.

Meanwhile, Hailey was smiling at him. "Looks like she takes after you," she said, nodding at Julie. Then, as he looked at her quizzically, she explained, "Patient."

Just then, Dillon held his hand up as the call was being answered.

"Maura?" he asked.

The first words out of the other woman's mouth were, "Did you find her?"

"Yes, Julie's here." He put his arm around Julie's slender shoulders and hugged her to him as he continued to talk to Maura. "She turned up on—my doorstep," he said, changing what he was about to say at the last minute. There was no point adding fuel to the fire and saying that the girl had appeared on Hailey's doorstep, he thought.

"Is she all right?" Maura asked, her voice catching.

He could tell Julie's mother was crying. He didn't ever remember hearing Maura cry. "She's fine, Maura," he assured the woman kindly. "None the worse for her experience."

"Well, I am," Maura snapped, her voice practically choking because of the tears in her throat she was trying to suppress.

Dillon really didn't know what to say to that. Deciding that there was nothing he could say, he just moved on and told her, "We'll be taking the next available flight back to Fort Lauderdale to bring her home."

"We?" Maura questioned.

He knew what she could be like and he wasn't about to get into this with Maura right now.

"I've got to go now, Maura," he told her, promising, "I'll text you the details when I have them."

And with that, Dillon terminated the call before Julie's mother had a chance to tell him what she thought about this whole thing.

Chapter Eighteen

The second that Dillon ended the call to her mother, Julie immediately spoke up. "She's a real pain, isn't she?"

"Don't talk about your mother that way," Dillon told his daughter. A part of him shared some of Julie's frustration, but he wanted to bring about a reconciliation—not escalate the feud that was in progress.

She looked surprised and somewhat betrayed by his admonishment. "Why not?" she cried. "It's true! She won't listen to anyone, not even her husband and he's kind of a nice guy."

"Be that as it may," Dillon told her, "she is still your mother and deserves your respect."

He was really struggling to take the high moral ground, and it was hard. Because all of his arguments with Maura had only managed to get him excluded from Julie's life. It was hardly fair. And yet, he was her father—and he knew this was the right thing to do. For both mother and daughter.

Julie fisted her hands at her waist belligerently. "Why?" she wanted to know. "My mother certainly doesn't give me any respect—or you for that matter," the girl pointed out angrily. She was obviously trying her best to get him to side with her against her mother.

This wasn't going well, Hailey thought. Feeling Dillon could use some help, she decided to step in. Not all that long ago, she could remember feeling exactly the same way that Julie was feeling right now, so she could easily commiserate with the preteen.

"That's one of those things that makes absolutely no sense now, but eventually, it will. I promise," she told Julie. "Trust me on that," Hailey added kindly.

Julie scowled at the two adults who were looking at her. "Well, I think you're wrong," she told them, obviously angry that things weren't turning out the way she had hoped.

"And you are entitled to think that way," Hailey told her, surprising both Julie and Dillon with her answer. "But not long ago I was exactly where you are right now. I was positive that everyone was against me—but they really weren't. As a matter of fact, one of those people gave me some very good advice. They said that sometimes a little bit of diplomacy goes a long way."

Hailey slipped her arm around the girl's shoulders. Julie stiffened, but Hailey left her arm where it was and after a moment, the girl began to relent.

"What you have before you is the long-term plan, not just something for the short haul. You need to try to get along with your mother and then maybe, eventually, she'll come around to your way of thinking. But she definitely won't come around if you insist on defying her and behaving like you can't stand her." She looked into the girl's eyes, searching for a glimmer to indicate that she had gotten through to Julie. "Do you understand what I'm saying to you?" Hailey asked her gently.

Julie sighed dramatically. "Yeah. I'm going back home," she answered, unhappy with this turn of events, but resigned.

"Yes, you are," Hailey agreed, glancing at Dillon. "And in exchange, your dad's going to try to convince your mom to allow him to visit you."

"And I won't stop until I convince her," Dillon promised.

Julie looked really skeptical, but Dillon thought that he could see a trace of hope taking root. "You think so?" the girl asked, looking from Dillon to Hailey.

"Absolutely," he told Julie. And then he looked around the immediate area. Julie hadn't arrived much before he had, so he reasoned she couldn't have put her suitcase away yet. "Where's your stuff?" he asked her.

Julie shrugged. "I didn't bring anything," she confessed.

Dillon thought he'd misunderstood. "You didn't bring a suitcase with you?"

"No," she answered. "I didn't want to attract any attention."

Amazed, Hailey turned her head away from Dillon and whispered, "You have one very sharp little girl on your hands. Most twelve-year-olds wouldn't have thought things through to this extent."

"I'm going to make reservations for the three of us," he told them, starting to take his credit card out of his wallet.

"The three of us?" Julie asked.

Dillon didn't miss the fact that his daughter sounded decidedly a great deal more hopeful. Even if she hadn't, he had no intentions of losing an ally at this crucial juncture. He knew he was going to need all the help he could get with Julie. Not just to get her home but also to find a way to entrench himself on the girl's good side and stay there.

And then, of course, there was the matter of being able to handle Maura once he got to Fort Lauderdale. This was going to be a challenge all around and he was going to need backup.

"You heard me," Dillon said. "The three of us." And then he finally turned away to make that call to whatever airline had the first available flight from here to Fort Lauderdale.

"Looks like you're going to get to meet my mother," Julie said, looking at Hailey. The girl didn't exactly sound as if she was happy about the prospect of seeing her mother again. "Now you get to see what I've had to put up with all these years," she predicted, followed by another deep sigh.

"Funny thing," Hailey told the girl, "your mother would probably say the same thing if anyone asked her how she felt about living with you."

Julie looked surprised by what Hailey said, then visibly upset. Julie's eyes closed into laser-like slits. "If she feels that way, then why won't she just let me go and live with my dad?"

"Because under all that arguing and rule-setting, your mother really loves you," Hailey told her. Julie's frown only grew deeper. Hailey had to bite her lip not to laugh. "Don't worry, this will all make sense to you in another fifty years. Or so."

"Fifty years?" Julie cried, stunned.

This time Hailey did laugh. "I'm just kidding, honey."

Julie's frown instantly intensified, then after a beat, grew a little less so. Tossing her head, she claimed dismissively, "I knew that."

"Okay, all set," Dillon announced, returning to the room. "We lucked out. A party of four just canceled their reservations. That's one more seat than we need."

"Maybe them canceling is an omen and we shouldn't go," Julie said, speaking up.

"Nice try," Dillon said with a laugh. "Okay, we need to get to the airport right now," he urged, and then he paused as he looked in Hailey's direction. "You want to pack anything?" he asked, giving her the opportunity to get a suitcase.

"Just a smile," she answered, adding, "Something tells me I'm going to need it."

And that's when it hit him. He had just assumed she was coming with him. He hadn't even asked her. "Listen, I just took it for granted that you'd want to come along with Julie and me. But you don't have to if you'd rather not," he told her, trying to find a graceful way of telling Hailey she was under no obligation to come with them.

Hailey looked at him as if he had lost his mind. "You're going to need moral support. There's no way I'm about to let you go alone," she told him.

"Dad's not alone," Julie protested. She squared her shoulders. "He's got me."

"My mistake," Hailey quickly backtracked. "There's no way that I'm letting the two of you go alone. Better?" she asked, looking at Julie.

The girl smiled as she nodded her approval. "Better," she answered.

And then she spared her father a glance as they were about to leave the house. Walking by him, Julie lowered her voice so that only he could hear what she wanted to say to him.

"You know, Dad, I like Hailey. I think she's really nice." she whispered with a wink just as she went out the door.

Dillon stood staring after Julie for a long moment. His daughter's words of approval had left him utterly speechless.

A petite Maura was standing there, waiting for them in her driveway when Dillon, Hailey and Julie pulled up in the car Dillon had rented at the airport. Hailey found herself feeling sorry for the woman.

Maura looked like a very frightened mother who was doing her best not to break down. She still had circles under her eyes from crying and, in general, she looked as if she hadn't slept a wink in the two days since her daughter had run away.

Leaning in toward Julie, Dillon whispered, "Why don't you give her a hug, Julie? She looks like she could really use one. Your mom's been through a lot in the last forty-eight hours."

Glancing at the girl, Dillon thought that Julie looked as if she really wanted to. But at the same time, she looked very reluctant to admit that fact to anyone.

And then she shrugged carelessly. "I guess I can if it means so much to you," Julie said.

"It does," Dillon agreed, playing his part because he sensed that was what Julie wanted to hear.

This time Julie really did appear to have her doubts. "It does?" she asked, looking incredulously at her father.

"Absolutely," Dillon guaranteed, trying to coax her to take the first step. He needed to have Maura in a decent frame of mind if they were going to come to some sort of an agreement about Julie.

"Okay," Julie mumbled. "If it means that much to everybody, I'll give her a hug." She grimaced as she said the words.

The next moment, there was no more time left for any debates or waffling. Maura crossed the distance between herself and her daughter, threw her arms around the girl and hugged Julie close to her as she obviously struggled to keep from dissolving into a puddle of tears.

But after the hugging had passed, Maura looked angrily at her daughter.

"I thought something awful had happened to you, that you were dead, or—" Her voice broke and she was unable to continue for a minute.

"Maura, we brought her back the minute that she turned up. Anyone of us would have been worried sick in your place," Dillon assured Maura. He wanted her to realize that they weren't enemies in this, but on the same side.

Maura looked like she was resisting believing him, but then she must have reconsidered.

"Thank you," she said in a small voice. And then she looked at her daughter. "But you shouldn't have run away like that. Do you know what could have happened to you?" Maura's voice went up as she contemplated the full implications of what she had just asked.

"The important thing is that it didn't," Dillon said, trying to get her to focus on the positive aspect of this reunion.

Maura suddenly became aware that there was someone else at this reunion besides Julie and Dillon. She glared at Hailey, then turned toward Dillon. "I'm sorry, who's this?" Maura asked coldly.

"This is Hailey Miller, Mom," Julie said, doing the introductions before her father could say anything. The girl smiled as she continued. "She's in charge of the wellness spa that Dad built."

"She's also the reason that I was able to get Julie to come back to Fort Lauderdale instead of having her run off again," Dillon told Maura.

Maura's expression was difficult to read as she looked between Julie and Hailey.

"Really? Julie, is this true?" Maura asked her daughter.

"I was pretty angry at you," the girl freely admitted, not attempting to hide the fact. "Some of my friends don't even have dads. I have one and you wouldn't even let me meet him no matter how much I begged you. So I decided to do it on my own," she said, a little defiantly.

"She's your daughter, all right," Dillon said without any intended malice. "Headstrong to a fault."

Maura's eyes narrowed. "Are you trying to insult me?"

"No, in his own way, he's giving you a compliment," Hailey told her, playing peacemaker again.

"It takes a strong, determined woman to raise a child on her own. If you hadn't been as strong as you were, you might not have been able to make it. Or to go on to marry someone you fell in love with," Hailey pointed out.

"Huh," was Maura's only initial comment.

She looked at Hailey for a long moment, silently going over things in her mind. And then she nodded her head, as if agreeing with the conclusion she had come to. Pulling her shoulders back, she said, "Would you like to come inside for some coffee?" she asked. Then, realizing that her question could be construed as only including one of them, Maura clarified, "Both of you."

"Are you sure?" Hailey asked, glancing toward Dillon to see if he was all right with this, as well.

"I wouldn't have asked you if I wasn't," Maura informed her pointedly.

"Well then, I'd love to come in for coffee. Our flight back to Texas isn't for several hours," she told Maura. She looked at Dillon. "How do you feel about coffee?"

"Definitely for it," he answered, following the two women and his daughter into the house. For the time being, peace appeared to have been restored, mostly, he thought, thanks to Hailey.

Chapter Nineteen

Dillon found himself anticipating an explosion, or at the very least, name-calling when the initial dust had settled, but neither scenario materialized. Instead, he and Hailey wound up having an exceedingly civilized visit with Maura, who, it seemed, had actually had time to think the situation over. The woman grudgingly agreed that perhaps allowing Dillon to have regular visits with their daughter was actually for the best.

By the time he and Hailey were at the airport, Dillon finally had to admit that things were beginning to look positively rosy.

"That was really a surprise," Dillon said to Hailey—not for the first time—as they began boarding their flight. "I honestly didn't think that Maura would ever actually come around." He couldn't believe the amount of relief he was experiencing.

Hailey waited until they had made their way to their seats and sat down before she commented. It didn't seem like the sort of conversation Dillon would appreciate having over the heads of strangers.

As she took her seat, she smiled at Dillon. She didn't know how he had managed to get them seats next to one another at the last minute, but he had.

"How could Maura not come around?" she asked him. "She's a mother, first and foremost," Hailey pointed out. "And when Julie ran away, I think it finally hit Maura just how much her daughter was being hurt by this war she was waging against you. If Maura didn't want to risk losing Julie again—or permanently—she knew she was going to have to change her tactics. In essence, Maura realized that she was going to have to loosen up," Hailey told him.

Dillon nodded. What Hailey was saying made sense. But he knew from experience that sense and Maura didn't always travel in the same circles.

"Still, this could have easily gone another way entirely," Dillon told her.

That sort of mindset could suck him down a dark rabbit hole, Hailey thought. She did what she could to block it.

"Don't think about what *could have* happened, just think about what did—and build on that," Hailey advised with an encouraging smile.

He looked reluctant for a moment—because it left him open to disappointment—but then he gave in.

"You're right," Dillon agreed, his mind already considering possibilities. "When this project is finally finished and behind me, I'm finally going to be able to start spending quality time with Julie."

And less time with me.

Well, what had she expected was going to happen? she asked herself. This was what Dillon had wanted, and in her own way, she had helped to bring about this scenario and make it happen.

While she was really glad for Dillon, Hailey couldn't help feeling sorry for herself.

And that was when it hit her.

She had fallen in love with Dillon.

There was no other reason why she wanted him to be happy in a situation that didn't include her. In order for him to be happy, he needed to spend time with Julie. What it boiled down to, she thought with a sinking heart, was that Dillon was going to be moving back to Fort Lauderdale when his jobs in Rambling Rose were finally wrapped up. Or maybe even before then.

He hadn't said anything about her moving there with him, but even if he had, Hailey thought, it was a hell of a chance for her to take, uprooting her whole life and resettling in Fort Lauderdale on the slim chance that Dillon *might* eventually propose to her.

What if he said he only wanted her to live with him, not marry him? Could she settle for that? Would she be happy with just that?

The empty feeling in the pit of her stomach was her answer.

No, she wouldn't.

Dillon looked at her. "You're being awfully quiet," he commented after ten minutes had passed.

She wasn't about to ruin this for Dillon by doing what she had told him not to do: focusing only on the negative side.

So she said brightly, "I'm just happy for you with how things turned out."

Dillon wasn't really buying that, but for now he nodded. "That's mostly thanks to your doing," he acknowledged. "If you hadn't told me to just hang in there…"

Hailey laughed, shaking her head. "Like someone could have actually bullied you into doing something," she told Dillon, stressing how inconceivable that was given the situation. "Accept the credit where it's due, Dillon. *You* did this. Maura saw how much this meant to you, and, more importantly, how much it meant to Julie. Maura is no dummy. She had to have known that if she stood in your way, she'd be the loser in more ways than one. She would have alienated Julie and, more than likely, by taking a stand against you, she would have lost her daughter."

What Hailey was saying was all true, but there was something in her tone that Dillon found troubling. Something that said while she was happy for him, she wasn't happy in the absolute sense. Something was bothering her.

But he had never been the type to push, to try to burrow deeply beneath the surface. If something was bothering Hailey and she wanted him to know, she would tell him. It was strictly her choice. So he left it—and her—alone.

It wasn't as if he didn't have a lot to occupy his mind. He and his brothers still had the hotel to build, not to mention that the restaurant was in its final stages and some things needed to be reviewed. That would be Ashley, Nicole and Megan's department, he thought. He had taken precious time away from all that to bring his daughter back to Fort Lauderdale. The round trip there and back had eaten up more than a day and he knew he was going to have to explain that. While he was thrilled to have finally met Julie face to face, he couldn't help wondering how his family was going to react about his having kept his daughter a secret from them. He just hoped that they'd understand and ultimately welcome this new member of the family.

"What's wrong?" Hailey asked, looking at the perplexed expression on Dillon's face.

They'd finally landed back in Texas and, since they didn't have the added inconvenience of having to wait for their luggage, they were able to make their way to the parking lot with relative speed. Dillon had driven his own car to the airport and had left it parked there when they began their odyssey back to Fort Lauderdale.

Having gotten into the vehicle, Dillon hadn't started the car. Instead, he had placed a call to Callum to let him know he was back. When his call went to voice mail, he called Steven—with the same results. So he tried calling Stephanie. When *that* call went to voice mail, as well, he began to feel frustrated. It showed all over his face—and that had prompted Hailey's question.

"What's wrong is all the calls I just made aren't going through. Instead they're all going to voice mail," he complained. "Something's up."

He wondered if it had something to do with the restaurant project.

"Are you sure you're getting a busy signal?" Hailey asked. "Maybe there's a tower that's gone down for some reason. Service has really improved in the last year in Rambling Rose, but sometimes..."

"No," he said, holding his phone up just in case she was right. But he could see that he had most of the bars on his cell phone. That wasn't the problem. "I've got four out of five bars, so there's definitely a signal."

"But nobody's answering?" she guessed.

Dillon frowned, putting his cell phone on the console tray.

"No," he confirmed. "Nobody's answering. Something must be up," he repeated, adding, "Something that appears to be involving my whole family."

"Like what?" she asked. So far, she wasn't able to connect the dots and wondered what was running through Dillon's mind.

"Beats me. Look, I can drop you off at your place—" His mind racing, Dillon was already trying to plan for several contingencies.

Hailey's voice wedged its way into his thoughts. "Or you can take me to wherever you're going," she told him. He had already been through a lot these last couple of days and she wanted to be there to support him no matter what came up. "Why don't we go to your ranch and start there?" she suggested. "Someone should probably be there and they might be able to tell you what's going on—*if* there is anything going on," she qualified.

Well, he certainly couldn't argue with that, Dillon thought.

"It's worth a shot," he agreed.

"Any guesses?" Hailey asked as they pulled out of the airport parking lot.

"Not a clue," he said, frustration throbbing in his voice. And then he had a thought. "Unless the city council has decided to pull their support for the new hotel we're building."

That, he thought, was the worst-case scenario. But what other reason was there for this sudden silence on his family's part? He didn't want to entertain any dire thoughts.

"Don't go there yet," Hailey advised. Then, because she had learned what he was like, she decided to qualify her words. "At least not until you have to. Maybe there's another explanation for what's going on."

At least she fervently hoped so.

But neither one of them could even hazard a guess what that could possibly be.

When they got to the ranch, they found Callum there with the twins. But his wife, Becky, didn't seem to be anywhere in sight.

"Why aren't you answering your phone?" were the first words out of Dillon's mouth as he walked into the main section of the mansion.

Completely involved with the twins, Callum looked up, startled. "Sorry, I've been on the phone for a good part of the last couple of hours—at least when the twins let me talk," he amended. Callum looked a little overwhelmed at the moment.

"I left you a couple of voice-mail messages," Dillon told him.

The truth of it was, he had left a couple of messages on both his brothers' phones, as well as on Stephanie's. Since being unable to reach anyone in his family wasn't a usual occurrence, he had gotten really concerned.

Trying to keep one of the girls from leaving her artwork permanently scribbled on the coffee table, thanks to the crayon she had found, Callum was only partially paying attention to his brother.

"Sorry, I didn't see the messages," Callum confessed, confiscating the crayon.

That wasn't like his brother, Dillon thought. Even with his hands full, Callum could always multitask. His initial gut feeling had been right. Something *was* definitely wrong.

"Is there some kind of trouble at work?" he asked Callum.

Callum looked at him blankly. "What?" And then Dillon's question seemed to sink in. "No," he answered. "It's nothing at work."

Hailey interceded, taking Luna, the overactive twin, from him. Callum looked at her gratefully.

"Then what?" Dillon wanted to know. If there wasn't a problem at work, then what *was* going on?

"And where's Becky?" Hailey asked, wiping off traces of jam from the other twin's face. "I'm guessing from that really tired expression on your face, she's not here, is she?"

"Becky's at the hospital," Callum answered. "I'm pinch-hitting for the babysitter who had some kind of last-minute emergency."

There was something in Callum's voice that told Dillon this wasn't just a regular workday for Becky, either. He could swear there was agitation in the air.

Before he could ask again, Callum looked up

and frowned. "Eric brought Linus back to Rambling Rose to see the doctor."

"We already know that part," Dillon said. And then his expression grew more serious. "This isn't just about a cold, is it?" he asked, recalling that he'd heard Linus's dad was worried about the boy.

His brother shook his head. Picking up Sasha, the sticky twin, he began to wash off her face and hands with a wet towel.

"No, I really wish it was, but it's more serious than that. A great deal more serious," Callum emphasized.

Instantly concerned—not just because Linus was the tiny local celebrity, but because she, like everyone else in Rambling Rose, had fallen in love with the boy—Hailey wanted to hear more details.

"Why, what's wrong with him, Callum?"

"According to Becky, a great deal. The upshot of it is that the kid might need a bone marrow transplant," Callum said.

As he spoke, he looked at the twins. Hailey could only imagine how he felt. He'd come to love those little girls in a short amount of time. How would he feel if it were one of the twins who was sick? She knew Callum's empathy as well as his heart went out to Linus's father. And to Linus.

"The poor little guy," Hailey said, thinking of

the hurdles the baby had already gone through: being born prematurely, then abandoned by his mother, who was still missing. It was just pure luck that his father had turned up. When they had broken up, Eric hadn't even known that Laurel was pregnant. He certainly hadn't been prepared to have her take off the way she had. The moment he'd found out what was going on, he had claimed Linus and then taken the boy with him.

And now this.

It just seemed like neither Linus nor his dad could catch a break.

"Well, Linus is rather young," Dillon said, thinking of the surgery. "But his dad's probably a match," he speculated, trying to think positive.

Callum picked up one of the girls and held her in his arms.

"Eric's at the hospital being tested right now," he told them. "If everything's okay, they'll confirm the diagnosis, and then the hospital can begin making preparations to do the surgery as soon as possible."

Hailey nodded. "The sooner the better," she agreed. "You don't want to wait too long. Some other complication might just crop up and then there might be more problems to deal with."

Dillon looked at her, curious. "How do you know so much about the subject?"

"I had a friend once who got very sick. The doctors thought it might be a problem with her bone marrow—but it wasn't." Hailey shrugged, realizing that she had gotten way too serious, reliving one of the attempts that had been made to save Janelle's life.

Clearing her throat, she deliberately forced a smile to her lips. "But that isn't going to happen with Linus. Like you said, his dad's probably a match and they'll do the transplant right away."

As if to bail her out, Callum's cell phone rang. Hailey took the twin he was holding into her own arms, along with the one she was already holding, to allow him to take the call in relative peace. Or that was her reasoning at the time.

Opening his phone, Callum saw that it was his wife calling. "Hi, honey, we were just talking about you." He glanced at his brother. Hailey guessed that Becky had probably just asked him who *we* were.

The next second, she saw that she was right because Callum told his wife, "Dillon and Hailey. They're back and I think—wait, what?"

Callum's entire countenance changed as he listened to his wife's voice on the other end of the call.

Hailey kept her eyes on him, taking everything in as all sorts of half thoughts were forming in her head.

Something more was obviously going on, she thought. Did it have to do with Linus?

Whatever it was, it couldn't be good. The expression on Callum's face was exceedingly serious and almost forbidding.

She and Dillon didn't have long to wait to find out. Ending the call, Callum put his phone back into his pocket as he looked from Dillon to Hailey.

"Well?" Dillon demanded. "What's going on?"

"Eric's not a genetic match to Linus," Callum told them in a quiet voice.

Chapter Twenty

For a moment, the only sounds in the room were the noises made by the twins as they babbled to each other. Dillon and Hailey looked at one another and then at Callum. Neither of them looked as if they could believe what they were hearing.

"What did you just say?" Dillon asked his brother in disbelief.

"Eric's not a match. He can't donate bone marrow to Linus."

"How is that possible?" Dillon wanted to know, confused.

"Well, just because Eric's his father doesn't necessarily mean that his bone marrow would be a match to Linus's. As a matter of fact, there could be a number of reasons why it doesn't match—" Hailey began to explain.

For the second time in less than two minutes, the only sounds that were heard were those being made by the twins as they were jabbering.

Callum shrugged helplessly. "Hey, I'm just repeating what Becky told me." He grabbed Sasha just as the twin was about to pull a throw pillow down from the sofa.

"Are they sure?" Hailey asked him, stunned.

"Oh, they're sure. When he wasn't a match for Linus's bone marrow, Eric insisted on a DNA test. He's on pins and needles until the results come through, but that's not going to be for a while," he told them, setting Sasha down away from anything she could pull on herself. "According to Becky, Eric's reeling. He's terrified for Linus's health." Callum's voice trailed off as he shrugged again.

As shocking as this news was, that wasn't what they should be focusing on right now, Hailey thought.

"Not all parents are immediate genetic matches when it comes to their kids. That's something to be looked into later," she said to the two brothers. "Right now the important thing is to find a bone marrow donor who's a match for Linus." There appeared to be only one solution. She looked from one brother to the other. "We've got to get the word out right away so volunteers can come in and be tested as soon as possible. If Linus is as sick as the doctor says, we can't afford to waste too much time." Her voice rose with each word she uttered.

"I agree," Dillon said, thinking how he would feel if this was Julie who needed to have a bone marrow transplant. A thought occurred to him. "I'll call Steven. Since he's married to the mayor, he can tell her all about this latest development. It's a given that Ellie will want to help," he said. "She can hold a press conference and make an announcement." He looked from his brother to Hailey to see if they agreed with him. "The way I see it, that would be the fastest way to get the word out. We could also send out emails to all the people who were invited to the spa's opening. The more people notified, the better."

Hailey nodded. "And I can have part of the spa close down tomorrow. We can hold the drive there," she told them. "We'll have all the volunteers come to the spa so they can be tested to see if any of them can be a donor. There's got to be a match for little Linus here somewhere," she insisted.

Callum nodded, eager to get started. "I'll call Becky back, let her know that all this is going on. That way she can get a team together to come over to the spa and bring everything they need to conduct the tests." Callum grinned, pleased as he looked at his brother and Hailey. "This is all really coming together fast," he commented as he began to redial his wife.

"I'll call Steven right now so he can get in contact with Ellie to tell her about this," Dillon said, taking out his phone, as well. "He might need time to get through if she's busy or in a meeting."

Hailey nodded. "Once you talk to him, I need to get back to the spa. It might take some time to get ready to handle the influx of volunteers." She tried not to think about how sick the baby was and just focus on the positive side: that they'd find a way to help him. "Since this is for the town's littlest celebrity, I think we should be prepared for a lot of people coming in to be tested."

Both brothers were unable to answer her since they were each on the phone talking to the next link on their particular chain.

Putting the twin she'd been holding into the double-wide playpen beside her sister, Hailey placed her own call. Hers was to Candace, her assistant at the spa, to alert the woman of what was going on. She wanted Candace to be prepared for a large influx of people arriving at the wellness spa, possibly before the hour was up. It all depended on how quickly Ellie could get a press conference together.

The next day, it all went down in what felt like lightning speed. As soon as Steven was told what was going on, he immediately called his wife. Fortunately he got through right away and was able to let her know about Linus and the baby's need for a bone marrow transplant. Ellie quickly called a press conference. Word spread from there like wildfire.

Meanwhile, right after Callum called her, Becky notified Dr. Green, the baby's doctor, about the bone marrow drive being organized at the spa. They lost no time putting together a team to test the volunteers that they anticipated coming in.

As soon as he had called Steven, Dillon drove Hailey directly to the spa. Her assistant was waiting for her and Hailey got right to work.

With the help of several of her people, plus Dillon, Hailey prepared one of the spa's larger rooms to be used for the necessary tests.

For inspiration, Hailey had a photograph of Baby Linus enlarged and taped up on the wall. Hailey felt that ignoring that sweet face was impossible. The more volunteers who came, the better the odds of finding a match.

Hailey moved the massage tables as well as chairs into the spacious room. They would need as many places as possible for volunteers to sit on as they waited for their turn to be swabbed.

Hailey and her people were still in the process of setting everything up when the first volunteers began arriving.

At the head of the line was a soft-spoken burly giant of a man named Riley Evans.

"I heard Mayor Ellie say that the baby was sick and could die if he didn't get something he needed. So I came to see if I could help," Riley told her without any fanfare.

Impressed with how quickly Riley had come down to the spa, Hailey still felt she had to ask the gentle giant, "Do you know what you'll be getting swabbed for today? What you might be donating?"

Riley shook his head. "Doesn't matter," he told her. "If I'm a match, you can have it if it'll help. Way I see it, the little guy's been through a lot and he needs whatever it is a lot more than I do."

Hailey found herself blinking back tears as she led Riley to a massage table.

As the crowd continued to gather and converge in and around the spa, that was the spirit that prevailed through it. Everyone was eager to do their part to try to help save Linus.

It quickly became apparent that almost *everyone* within the small close-knit town was volunteering to have their cheeks swabbed for matching.

The volunteers included Dillon and his two brothers.

"That was very nice of you," Hailey commented as Dillon got up off the table.

He rolled down his sleeve. "Hey, I couldn't very well just stand by while everyone else was being tested. Especially now that I know what it feels like to be a parent, I totally empathize with that situation." He laughed softly to himself. "In a way, since the moment he came into the world, I guess Linus belongs to everyone. Especially since his mother took off and left him." Dillon looked at Hailey to see if she agreed with him.

She thought about the sentiment he had just voiced. "I didn't realize you felt that way," she told him. "I mean, when we were flying to Fort Lauderdale, I thought you made it pretty clear that you considered that home, not Rambling Rose."

He thought back for a moment. "I guess, at the time, I did," he admitted.

At the time.

Did that mean that now he didn't? Before she could stop herself, she asked him.

"And now?"

The moment the words were out of her mouth, Hailey knew she might wind up regretting pushing this. In all honesty, she knew that it was probably better if she just left this alone and let whatever happened progress at its own speed.

But there was another part of her that felt as if she was just deliberately stalling, trying to hold back the inevitable.

That wasn't like her.

She needed to know what was ahead. If she was going to lose Dillon, then she needed to know that, too. She shouldn't be embarrassing herself by desperately trying to hold on when there was no chance for her.

For them.

"And now I can see that no matter what your plans are," Dillon was saying to her, "the universe can be totally unfair. There are no guarantees in life, other than the fact that it's completely uncertain and can all change in the blink of an eye."

Here it came, Hailey thought, trying to mentally brace herself.

But all she could focus on was that her stomach felt as if it were sinking as she waited for Dillon to utter the fatal words that would take him away from her. He was going to tell her that he'd decided not to wait until his part of the project was done. That he intended to go back to Florida as soon as possible.

A wave of heat passed over her as her pulse began to race.

Although it went against what she told herself she should do, Hailey heard herself tell Dillon, "You can't just give up like that, Dillon."

That stopped him cold.

"Give up?" Dillon repeated.

He sounded confused, Hailey thought. As if he didn't know what she was talking about.

Hailey went right on talking as if he hadn't said a word. "You can't," she insisted. "Growing up, I had a friend, Janelle, who was closer to me than my own sister. We did *everything* together and she had such a zest for life! Janelle could always lift me up no matter how bad things seemed. No matter how down I was feeling." She smiled, remembering. "We were going to conquer the world together once we graduated from school."

Dillon couldn't imagine tragedy touching this sunny woman before him. "What happened?" he asked quietly.

Hailey sighed. "The world conquered her. Or at least it tried to," she amended. "Janelle was diagnosed with pancreatic cancer, but she never gave in to it, never let it get her down. She fought it right to the very end. She was my inspiration and she made me promise that no matter what, I would always live life to the fullest. For both of us," she added emotionally. "Because of her, I learned that you have to grab every single thing that life has to offer and make the very most of it because tomorrow, it could all just disappear."

Dillon nodded. "I know."

"You know?" she questioned, confused.

Did that mean he'd decided to stay in Rambling Rose? Or was he saying that was the reason he'd decided to leave?

Her mind was jumping around from one thought to another and her head was beginning to ache. Hailey forced herself to stop, to wait for Dillon to tell her what he intended to do.

"Yes, I do. I get it," he told her. "Life is short, much too short. And I don't want to get caught up in all the tiny details and let that get in the way so that I'm wasting time wading through it. Unscrambling the small stuff and not paying attention to the really important things."

Breathe, Hailey, breathe! Maybe Dillon wasn't saying he was leaving. Maybe he was—

No, no more jumping to conclusions. Let him talk.

"Maybe I'm not saying this right," Dillon continued, a little exasperated. "Actually, I know I'm not—"

This was her chance to stop him, she thought.

Hailey grabbed it. "Maybe you should wait then, until you feel you have the right words. No point in rushing this," she told him.

Especially since you can always say goodbye. At the thought, another strong wave of nausea assaulted her stomach.

This was about finding a bone marrow donor for Linus, not about promoting her romance, she upbraided herself. How could she be so self-centered?

And yet…

Lost in thought and trying very hard to rally, she didn't realize what Dillon was doing until he had dropped down on one knee and taken her hand.

"Hailey," he began.

Stunned, Hailey's mouth dropped open. "What are you doing?" she cried.

"Probably making a huge fool of myself," Dillon guessed. "But I don't seem to have a choice in the matter."

Her breath was backing up in her throat again and her heart was doing an imitation of a jackhammer as she continued to stare at Dillon.

Was he—?

It couldn't be—and yet—

"Dillon?" she questioned uncertainly.

They were attracting attention now, but at this point, she could only see the rugged man before her down on one knee.

"I know that I'm more frog than prince and you do deserve a prince of the highest caliber, but I promise you that if you'll have me, if you say yes, I will love you with all my heart for as long as we both shall live. Longer," he added with feeling. "All I want is the chance to show you.

"But I'll understand if you decide to turn me down, although—"

"Dillon," Hailey cried, desperately trying to get a word in edgewise.

Ready to go on full steam ahead, he stopped abruptly. "What?"

"Stop talking!" she told him.

He thought she was telling him that to save him any further embarrassment.

"So it's no?" he asked, trying to brace himself for defeat.

"No, you big dumb oaf," she laughed. "Stop talking so I can say yes."

"Yes?" He repeated the word as if he didn't understand what she was telling him.

Suppressing a laugh, Hailey spelled it out for him. "Yes, I will marry you."

His eyes widened. "You will?"

"Yes," she cried again, then, for good measure, before he could question her reasoning, she added, "Because I love you."

"You do?" he said it as if he didn't believe that was possible.

"Yes. I've loved you ever since you spilled that jasmine on your shirt and then had a sneezing fit." Her eyes were shining now. "You obviously needed someone in your life. I decided that you needed me," Hailey told him, smiling broadly.

"But—"

She decided that the only way she was going to get Dillon to stop arguing and accept the answer he had made clear he wanted was to take matters into her own hands.

Or, in this case, it wasn't her hands that she used, it was her lips.

She pressed them on his and whatever else Dillon was about to say just faded away.

Happily.

Neither one of them heard the volunteers around them cheering. They were far too busy forming their own little world.

* * * * *

WE HOPE YOU ENJOYED
THIS BOOK FROM

HARLEQUIN
SPECIAL
EDITION

Believe in love. Overcome obstacles. Find happiness.

Relate to finding comfort and strength in the
support of loved ones and enjoy the journey
no matter what life throws your way.

6 NEW BOOKS AVAILABLE EVERY MONTH!

COMING NEXT MONTH FROM

⊕ HARLEQUIN

SPECIAL EDITION

Available April 21, 2020

#2761 BETTING ON A FORTUNE
The Fortunes of Texas: Rambling Rose • by Nancy Robards Thompson
Ashley Fortune is furious Rodrigo Mendoza has been hired to consult on her new restaurant and vows to send him packing. Soon her resentment turns to attraction, but Rodrigo won't mix business with pleasure. When her sister gives her a self-help book that promises to win him over in a week, Ashley goes all in to land Rodrigo's heart!

#2762 THEIR SECRET SUMMER FAMILY
The Bravos of Valentine Bay • by Christine Rimmer
Officer Dante Santangelo doesn't "do" relationships, but the busy single dad happily agrees to a secret summer fling with younger, free-spirited Gracie Bravo. It's the perfect arrangement. Until Gracie falls for Dante, his adorable twins and their ever-present fur baby!

#2763 HER SECOND FOREVER
The Brands of Montana • by Joanna Sims
The car accident that left her permanently injured made Lee Macbeth only more determined to help others with disabilities. Now there's a charming cowboy doing a stint of community service at her therapeutic riding facility and he wants more from the self-sufficient widow. Despite their powerful mutual attraction, Lee won't risk falling for Mr. Totally Wrong...will she?

#2764 STARTING OVER IN WICKHAM FALLS
Wickham Falls Weddings • by Rochelle Alers
Georgina Powell is finally moving out of her parents' house after years of carrying her mother's grief. At thirty-two years old, she's ready for a fresh start. She just didn't expect it to come in the form of Langston Cooper, the famed war correspondent who recently returned to buy Wickham Falls's local paper. But as she opens her own business, his role as editor in chief may steer him in a different direction—away from their future together.

#2765 THE RELUCTANT FIANCÉE
The Taylor Triplets • by Lynne Marshall
When Brynne Taylor breaks off her engagement to Paul Capriati, she knows her life is going to change. But when two women who claim to be triplets to her show up in her small Utah town, it's a lot more change than she ever expected. Now she's digging up long-buried family secrets and navigating her relationship with her ex-fiancé. Does she actually want to get married?

#2766 THE NANNY'S FAMILY WISH
The Culhanes of Cedar River • by Helen Lacey
Annie Jamison has dreamed of capturing the heart of David Culhane McCall. But she knows the workaholic widower sees her only as a caregiver to his children. Until her resignation lands on his desk and forces him to acknowledge that she's more than just the nanny to him. Is he ready to risk his heart and build a new family?

"Gracie, will you look at me?"

Stifling a sigh, she turned her head to face him. Those melty brown eyes were full of self-recrimination and regret.

"I'm sorry," he said. "I never should have touched you. I'm too old for you, and I'm not any kind of relationship material, anyway. I don't know what got into me, but I swear to you it's never going to happen again."

Hmm. How to respond?

Too bad there wasn't a large blunt object nearby. The guy deserved a hard bop on the head. What was wrong with him? No wonder it hadn't worked out with Marjorie. The man didn't have a clue.

But never mind. Gracie held it together as he apologized some more. She watched that beautiful mouth move and pondered the mystery of how such a great guy could have his head so far up his own ass.

Maybe if she yanked him close and kissed him, he'd get over himself and admit that last night had been amazing, the two of them had off-the-charts chemistry and he didn't want to walk away from all that goodness, after all.

Yeah, kissing him might shut him up and get him back on track for more hot sexy times. It had worked more than once already.

But come on. She couldn't go jumping on him and smashing her mouth on his every time he started beating himself up for having a good time with her.

No. A girl had to have a little pride.

He thought last night was a mistake?

Fair enough. She'd actually let herself believe for a minute or two there that they had something good going on, that her long dry spell manwise might be over.

But never mind about that. Let him have it his way. She would agree with him.

And then she would show him exactly what he was missing. And then, when he couldn't take it anymore and begged her for another chance, she would say that they couldn't, that he was too old for her and it wouldn't be right.

Don't miss
Their Secret Summer Family *by Christine Rimmer,*
available May 2020 wherever
Harlequin Special Edition books and ebooks are sold.

Harlequin.com

Get 4 FREE REWARDS!

We'll send you 2 FREE Books plus <u>2</u> FREE Mystery Gifts.

Harlequin Special Edition books relate to finding comfort and strength in the support of loved ones and enjoying the journey no matter what life throws your way.

FREE Value Over **$20**